A TALE OF TWO ENEMIES

A LITERATIA NOVEL

G. LEESON

GRACE ABRAHAM PUBLISHING

Grace Abraham Publishing
A Division of Washington Cooper, Inc.
13335 Holbrook St., Suite 10
Bristol, Virginia 24202

Publisher's note: This is a work of fiction. Names, characters, places, and incidents are a product of the author's imagination. Locales and public names are sometimes used for atmospheric purposes. Any resemblance to persons living or dead, or to businesses, companies, events, institutions, or locales is completely coincidental.

Book Cover Design 2023 by Cover Villain.

Ordering information:
Special discounts are available on quantity purchases by corporations, associations, and others. For details, contact the "Special Sales Department" at the above address.

An Eyre of Mystery/G. Leeson – First edition
ISBN: 978-1-7373009-7-7

A TALE OF TWO ENEMIES

CHAPTER 1

I was having lunch with my friend—the only person from college with whom I'd stayed in touch—and I was beginning to regret it. Don't get me wrong. I liked Connie. She was great. Plus, I had been incommunicado from everyone while I'd been taking care of my mother, so I felt I owed it to Connie, and maybe to myself, to spend some time catching up.

"So, what is it you do, Gia?" Connie gazed at me as she sipped her iced tea.

How could I possibly explain to her what I do? We were different people now. We moved in entirely different worlds. In fact, I moved between two.

Well, you see, Connie, I travel through a portal into a place called Literatia. In Literatia, there are silverfish trying to devour classic literature because—well, why would they not? I mean, some of those books are delicious, right? Anyway, they mess up the books, and I have to go in there, find this sweetie

3

pie named Matthew who's kinda trapped there and has been for decades, and together we put things right so that the book is saved. Why is it so important to save the books? Well, if they're destroyed in Literatia, they disappear from our world as if they'd never existed.

Obviously, I didn't say any of that because Connie either would've recommended a good therapist or fainted on the spot. I was guessing therapist. Instead, I said, "I'm an archivist at a manor home."

Connie wrinkled her nose as she sat her glass down. "Sounds boring...and dusty."

Chuckling, I said, "The house is anything but dusty, and I'm seldom bored."

"Really? Before leaving the office to come here, I was finalizing the paperwork for a hostile takeover worth twenty million dollars." Did I mention Connie was a corporate lawyer? And, come to think of it, she sounded as if she was becoming something of a snob. "What were *you* doing?"

I supposed the truth couldn't hurt in this case. "I was reading about the French Revolution."

"Ugh. All those people getting their heads chopped off? That sounds horrible."

"Not to me. I find it fascinating." Especially since I was likely getting ready to dive headfirst into *A Tale of Two Cities.* I used my fork to pick around in my salad. I'd already eaten all the best parts of it, but I hoped there might still be a bacon bit or a crouton to uncover.

The curator had recently heard some rumblings that

there had been more *worst of times* than *best of times* within *A Tale of Two Cities*. Granted, the book totally dwelled on those *worst of times* since it was all about Madame Defarge wanting Charles Darnay and his entire family sent to the guillotine because his father and uncle were responsible for the death of her sister. But this was different. This was silverfish-induced *worst of times.*

Connie shrugged. "I'm glad you like it." Her tone implied she'd rather have bamboo shards shoved under her fingernails. "Are you seeing anyone?"

"No." The man I was seeing—or, rather, wanted to see —was the aforementioned Matthew who was in Literatia, so a simple *no* would have to suffice. "You?"

"There's an attorney in our office who has asked me out a couple of times. He's cute, but if it didn't work out, I'd be stuck seeing him all the time unless one of us transferred. And I'm definitely not leaving. My career is really taking off."

"Still, I suppose you could go on one date and see if you have anything in common," I said.

"I don't know. I might." She took another drink. "Is there anyone you could set me up with? What about your boss? Is he handsome?"

"He is, but I don't think he's in the market for a girlfriend right now. Besides, he's old enough to be our dad." Hypocritical aside here, the guy I was crushing on was even older, but that was an entirely different circumstance. Time moved much slower in Literatia, so he wasn't—biologically speaking—all that old.

"Who cares? Is he rich?" she asked.

Reader, was there a nice way to say none of your business? If there was, it eluded me at that moment.

"Are you joking, or have you always been this shallow?" The words slipped out before I'd realized it. They hung there between us like an awkward, heavy chain stretching from my mouth to her ear. No way to reel them back in, so I forced out a laugh.

She laughed too. "You had me going there for a second!"

"You're so easy to tease!" My phone rang, and I said a silent prayer of thanksgiving. "I need to take this." I slid my chair back, stood, and walked out into the lobby of the restaurant. "Josephine, is everything okay?"

Josephine was the assistant to Cooper, the curator.

"I realize you're—" She sighed. "We need you back. As quickly as possible."

"I'm on my way." I returned to the table to tell Connie I had to go. "I'll pay the check on my way out."

"I won't hear of it. Lunch is on me." She made a shooing motion with both hands. "You hurry back to your French Revolution. I'm going to linger here for a few more minutes."

"All right." I bent and gave her a one-armed hug. "Thanks!" I hurried out of the restaurant. As eager as I was to see what was wrong at Smithmore Manor, I was even more keen on escaping this uncomfortable lunch.

I HURRIED into the library where Josephine, wearing white cotton gloves, was sitting on the sofa with the gilt-embossed copy of Charles Dickens' first edition *A Tale of Two Cities*. I'd been poring over the book a couple of days ago when there were only minor glitches in the story.

"What's happened?" I looked around the room. "Where's Cooper?"

"He went upstairs to lie down. He's not feeling well."

I sat beside her on the sofa. "Is whatever happened in the book that bad?" Opening my purse, I took out my own white cotton gloves and slipped them on so I could handle the book. I couldn't imagine anything worse than *Jane Eyre's* hero, Edward Rochester, being found guilty of his wife's murder; but that hadn't made Cooper take to his bed. That had only made him shove me into the deep end of the pool, so to speak, where I'd had to sink or swim.

"Dr. Manette has been murdered." With a sigh, Josephine closed the book and handed it to me.

"How—? When?" My questions were tumbling over each other in my head.

"I found the passage right before I called you. You're going to have to go into the book at once."

Sitting there cradling the book on my lap, I felt like an idiot. I had no idea how to travel to Literatia without Cooper. Heck, I didn't know how to go into the book *with* Cooper. I swallowed the lump in my throat. "Do you know how to get me there?"

She nodded. "I'm nowhere near as accomplished as

Cooper, but I can put you where you need to be. You'll be going in as Lucie Manette. Matthew is already there as Charles Darnay."

"My husband." I clamped my lips together. That was twice in less than an hour that I wished I'd kept my mouth shut. "I mean, where in the book are we?"

"Yes, you're married," she said, slipping off her gloves.

"Oh, good. That will make communication so much easier."

Seriously, Reader, my feelings had very little to do with being able to walk around with my arm hooked through his or being able to steal a chaste kiss now and then. It was hard for an unmarried woman to even speak with a man unchaperoned back in the day.

Ignoring my interruption, she continued. "You've had to forego your honeymoon due to the death of Lucie's father."

"Then neither of our characters killed him." I brightened. "That's nice to know."

Josephine rubbed the bridge of her nose. "Are you ready to go?"

I hesitated. Preparation hadn't been an option before I was sent into *Jane Eyre*. "Is there anything you feel I should know or that I should do?"

"Only to be careful, but you know that."

"Should I read about the murder? Do you think that would help?"

"There's not much to read. Miss Pross found the man

lying face down on the floor in the parlor," she said. "That's all we've got at this point."

"I'd like to see Cooper before I go." I placed the book on the side table before I took off my gloves and returned them to my purse. "Where's his room?"

She shook her head. "No. He needs his rest, and I won't have him disturbed. Besides, you have work to do."

Cooper had seemed fine this morning. And he was still relatively young. I'd never known him to go to bed sick. Granted, I'd only been here a short while.

"Does he have some sort of condition I'm not aware of?" I asked.

"He'll be fine. You need to go. Now."

"What do I need to do?" When I'd been transported into *Jane Eyre* by Cooper, I'd reached for a book, placed my hand on a glowing *L*, and found myself on a street in Victorian England not having a clue as to what was going on.

Josephine nodded toward the book lying on the table. A glowing *L* was now on the cover.

"Just put my hand on it?" I asked.

"Yes. Fingers crossed it's going to work."

Reader, it didn't work. Rather than getting ready to board a ship with my new husband, I found myself standing at the back of a small church wearing a rose-colored dress with a pouf skirt preparing to walk down the aisle on the arm of Dr. Manette!

CHAPTER 2

The wedding dress was lovely, and I was certain my appearance had been changed to resemble that of Lucie Manette. I'd asked Cooper upon my return from the world of *Jane Eyre* how I and everyone in Literatia had seen me as Jane. He'd chalked it up to "a little magic and a whole lot of ignorance." He'd said Literatia is primarily a world of fiction, so the characters see only what they want to see; and when I was a part of that world, I was also corrupted to an extent by the narrative. I knew who I was, but in *Jane Eyre*, I saw myself as Jane. Here in *A Tale of Two Cities,* my appearance would be that of Lucie Manette.

My thoughts continued to race as I walked slowly down the aisle. It wasn't too late to save Dr. Manette! This mission should be simple. All Matthew and I had to do was keep Dr. Manette alive and thwart his killer's plans. Then Cooper—or Josephine—would be able to pull both of us out of *A Tale of Two Cities*. What could go wrong?

Reader, never ever ask that question.

I glimpsed Charles Darnay standing at the front of the church. Oh, wow. The book had made me think the man was a looker, but...oh, wow. Was that *Matthew*? It had to be. Josephine said he was already here. But she'd planned to put me into the book *after* Dr. Manette was found murdered, so was it possible that the man at the front of the church was indeed the character Charles Darnay and not Matthew Wellingham?

Charles turned his head and smiled at me.

Oh, wow.

If that was Matthew, he was even more handsome as Charles than he had been as Edward. I had no idea what Matthew looked like out of character. Cooper had offered to show me a photo of him, but I'd declined. I wanted to wait until Matthew and I could see each other in person. It didn't seem fair for me to know what he looked like when he'd only known me as Jane Eyre and now as Lucie Manette. If that was, in fact, Matthew.

My steps faltered.

Dr. Manette gripped my arm tighter. "Are you all right, darling?"

I turned to him, warmed by the concern I saw on his face. "I'm fine, Father."

"You are certain of Charles?" he asked.

"Absolutely." I smiled.

At the end of the aisle, Dr. Manette handed me off to Charles Darnay. No—to Matthew. I knew as soon as I could gaze into his eyes.

"I've missed you," he whispered.

The butterflies in my stomach fluttered. "I've missed you too."

THE CEREMONY WAS OVER QUICKLY, and there was no "and now you may kiss the bride" recitation at the end of it. Charles slipped a gold band onto the ring finger of my left hand before bowing slightly and kissing the hand.

As we walked down the aisle to leave the church, I tried to think of a way to tell him we couldn't leave. There was no way to do that without drawing attention, so at the vestibule, I simply turned and faced the guests.

"Thank you all for being here and sharing this special day with us."

Some cheered, some murmured, and some looked at me with confusion. Dr. Manette, still at the front of the church, was one of the latter.

Sydney Carton—I knew it was him because he looked nearly identical to Charles Darnay—smirked at me from about midway up the aisle. I wondered what he was thinking. Was he wishing Lucie had chosen him over Charles? Maybe he believed Lucie was now regretting her decision.

Reader, if you've read A Tale of Two Cities *or seen any of the dramatizations, then you might see why Lucie would have been tempted to pick Sydney. I sure would have been. I mean, if a man tells you that you've been the last dream of his soul, he could very well be a keeper.*

"Father, come with us to the ship," I continued. "I'd love for you to see us off."

"Nonsense!" Miss Pross scurried toward me quicker than any woman her age should have been able. "I'll ride along with you."

"No. I want Father." I was making a fool of myself in front of all these people; but if my plan to keep Dr. Manette alive panned out, Matthew and I could hopefully laugh about it together soon at the manor in North Carolina.

Luckily for me, Matthew caught on and trusted there was a good reason for what I was doing. "Yes, Dr. Manette, please come to the dock and see us off."

Dr. Manette chuckled. "I see what you are both doing —you are making an old man feel he is still a necessary part of your family."

"You are!" I said.

"I know that, my sweet girl. Go on your honeymoon now. I will see you soon."

Before either Matthew or I could say anything else, Jarvis Lorry—a banker and friend of Dr. Manette— strode toward us and began turning us both toward the door.

"Go now, young couple. Your carriage is waiting," he said.

Other guests fell in behind Mr. Lorry and helped him usher us outside. I tried to turn to see Lucie's father, but there were too many people between us and Dr. Manette. Mr. Lorry was still near enough that I could speak to him.

"Mr. Lorry, please. My father needs me. What if he—"

"He'll be *fine*." Mr. Lorry clucked his tongue and shook his head. "Trust Miss Pross and me to look after him."

"Yes, but—"

Mr. Lorry opened the carriage door. He had a benevolent, closed mouth smile on his face. I stared at him, hoping that if he were a silverfish, one would slither through his lips so that I'd know before stepping up into the carriage. Silverfish in the teeth—that's how I'd known which characters were imposters when I'd visited the world of *Jane Eyre*.

Matthew bent his head to whisper to me, "Come on. We'll have the carriage turn around as soon as we're out of this crowd."

Nodding, I accepted his help getting into the carriage. *Reader, that was no easy task in a wedding dress from the 18th Century. Seriously, give it a go sometime if you don't believe me.*

He pulled the door closed, and the carriage started moving. I could hear the crowds cheering in the background. I sat back against the seat and inhaled the scents of horse, leather, and Matthew's cotton shirt.

I took a moment to appreciate this man, who looked like a fairy tale prince in his fancy embroidered coat, breeches, and silk hose. Smiling, I said, "You're—"

My words were interrupted with a proper kiss. I should've minded—Dr. Manette's life was hanging in the balance, after all—but I didn't. I kissed him back. We were going to return to the house, and surely no one would kill Dr. Manette in front of all those wedding guests, right?

"Oh, Mathew." I sighed. "I wish you could have come back with me before."

"From here on out, we must call each other *Charles* and *Lucie*," he said.

"Yeah, okay." The sweet greeting was over. Now it was time to get down to business and keep Dr. Manette alive. "What do you know?"

"I know there's to be a murder, but I don't know who or when."

"Well, it's Dr. Manette. That's why I didn't want to let him out of our sight. Josephine was supposed to send me into the book just before you and I boarded the ship, and we were to be called back because Dr. Manette was killed. Obviously, she was off. We still have time to save him."

"Josephine?" He frowned. "Why not Cooper?"

"He wasn't feeling well."

He searched my face. "Is there anything you aren't telling me?"

"All I know is that he wasn't feeling well and went to lie down," I said. "I wanted to go up and check on him, but Josephine said it was imperative that I go into the book at once, and she didn't want to disturb Cooper."

"Okay." He still appeared to be worried.

I squeezed his hand. "Cooper will be fine. I'm hoping you'll be in North Carolina to see that for yourself before you know it. All we have to do is get to Dr. Manette before his murderer does, and we're home free on this one."

"I'd love to think it will be that easy, but it never is."

"There's a first time for everything."

Charles reached out of the window and slapped his hand against the side of the carriage.

"Yes, sir?" the driver called.

"Take us to the Manette home at once!" He looked back at me and relaxed slightly. "I really have missed you. We were only beginning to get to know each other when you were taken away from me."

"At least, being a married couple, we won't have the impediments we had in *Jane Eyre*."

He laughed softly. "I like the sound of that."

I felt my face flame. "I meant that we'll be able to speak unchaperoned now."

"I knew what you meant. I just love to tease you." He gave me a quick peck on the lips. "Now, to save Dr.

Manette and not have our heads separated from our necks."

"Don't worry, it's too early in the book for that."

Arching a brow, he said, "Don't be too sure. You've seen how quickly circumstances change in a book once the silverfish get their teeth into it."

CHAPTER 3

Matthew…er…Charles….

Reader, I decided to refer to him as Charles even with you for now because I believed it would be easier for all of us that way.

Charles and I hurried into the house. I let out a breath and sank against him in relief when I saw Dr. Manette standing in the center of the salon. He was holding a glass of wine aloft as he talked with a group of men.

"Father!" I hurried over to him and took the glass from his hand. After all, we had no idea how he died—he might've been poisoned. "You know you need to look after your health."

"I do know that, dear. I'm a *doctor*, remember?" His smile was gentle, but the laughter of his friends stung a little. I mean, sure, I was acting like a brat, but I was trying to save the man's life.

"And yet you take care of everyone but yourself," I said.

"Is that why you've dragged poor Charles back here?" he asked. "You're afraid I'll die if left to fend for myself?"

Um…yeah, that was pretty much it in a nutshell.

Fortunately, Charles stepped in to help me out. "See how she fusses over you? She's going to make a wonderful mother."

"Anon, I hope," Dr. Manette said. "I'm eager to have a little one brightening up this house."

"Indeed!" Mr. Lorry already had enough wine in him to loosen his tongue. "Hobbeldygee back into that carriage else there'll be no marriage music around here!"

I frowned at Charles and mouthed, *What?*

Smiling at Mr. Lorry and Dr. Manette, he said, "Right you are," and pulled me to a corner of the room.

"What did he say?" I asked.

"He said for us to trot on back to the carriage or else there wouldn't be any babies around here."

Rolling my eyes, I huffed. "As if we'd need to go on a trip to make a—"

Charles gently stopped my words with an index finger over my lips. "Not so loud." He grinned. "I mean, hold that thought, but first things first."

I felt a blush creeping into my cheeks. "What do we do now?"

"I'll get him alone and convince him to go with us."

"All right." I watched Charles make his way back into

the semi-circle of men standing with Dr. Manette until my attention was diverted by a voice at my side.

"Lucie."

I turned to see Sydney Carton with his bedroom eyes boring into mine.

Reader, I gulped. I'd had a literary crush on Sydney Carton since I'd first read A Tale of Two Cities *years ago. Yes, he looked identical to Charles, but there was something a little more dangerous about Sydney—something more passionate.*

"Sydney." The word emerged as a whisper, practically of its own volition.

"Having second thoughts?" His voice was low and quiet, and I felt his breath on my neck as he leaned closer to make himself heard.

"About what?"

He laughed softly. "Your marriage."

"Oh! That! Yes. I mean, *no*. No, I'm not having second thoughts. It's just that I don't want to leave my father unattended."

"I don't believe you. You know your father will be fine if you go on your honeymoon," he said. "Miss Pross is here. Mr. Lorry will also look in on him, as will I." He moved slightly, putting himself between me and the rest of the room. "Tell me you've made a mistake, and I'll immediately have this marriage annulled."

I tried to see around him, but he was rather broad and moved with me. "Please. I need to see my father."

"You want to seek his counsel?" Sydney asked.

"No." I brought my eyes back to his face—his beautiful face. "I'm…" I took a deep breath. "I'm happy with Charles. It's my father I'm concerned about."

"I still don't believe you," he said.

Shrugging slightly, I said, "I can't help what you do or don't believe. Excuse me." I stepped around him only to realize I'd lost sight of both Charles and Dr. Manette. Where had they gone?

I spotted a woman who looked as if she'd be gossipy —she was bony and dressed in black. Her small, alert eyes and the manner in which she bobbed her head this way and that made me think of her as a blackbird.

Sitting beside her on the settee, I said, "I hope you're having a nice time."

"Nice enough." Those beady eyes scanned me up and down. "And why aren't you on a ship by now?"

"I was worried about my father," I said. "I realize it seems silly, but we—" My mind raced for a logical reason for a grown woman to be so paranoid about leaving her dad to go on her honeymoon. The answer was in the original plot of the book.

Dr. Manette had been imprisoned in the Bastille in France when *A Tale of Two Cities* opened, and Lucie had believed herself to be an orphan. Mr. Lorry had taken Lucie to France where Monsieur Defarge was keeping the insane doctor in a garret. Lucie's love and devotion apparently made him well again.

"I imagine you know my father had a terrible time of it in France," I said to Blackbird.

"I do." She smiled, and there it was—a silverfish darted through her teeth.

Managing to suppress a shiver, I said, "Then perhaps you understand why I'm reluctant to leave him. Have you seen him lately? He was talking with a group of men earlier, but I don't see him now."

"I believe it's just as well that you don't."

I quickly stood, intending to search every room in the house if I had to. I didn't have to. Miss Pross' scream ripped through the house from the direction of the kitchen. But Josephine said Miss Pross had found Dr. Manette in the parlor. Of course, at that time, Charles and I had been at the dock.

"No." I said the word under my breath, but I heard Blackbird chuckle softly before I sprinted to the kitchen.

Miss Pross stood over the body of Dr. Manette, who'd apparently been struck on the head with a cast iron cooking pot. The pot lay on the floor, and the kitchen door was standing open.

Closing my eyes against the sight of the poor man lying there in a puddle of blood, I felt strong hands grip my shoulders. When I opened my eyes and turned to see that the hands belonged to Charles, I sagged in regret.

"I'm sorry," I whispered.

"Are you going to faint?" he asked.

"No."

"Good. I'm going after the killer." He stepped around the body and went out the door.

"Let me through," an older man with a doctor's bag said. "I'm an old friend and colleague of Dr. Manette."

As the doctor was examining Dr. Manette, Mr. Lorry and Sydney Carton skirted past me and out the door. Charles and the other two men returned just as the older man—presumably a physician—was declaring Dr. Manette dead.

"I've sent for the constable," Miss Pross said.

"I'll take one more look around the alleys and streets to ask if anyone saw a man fleeing the Manette house," Sydney said.

A few other men accompanied him, but Charles said, "I'm going to take my wife upstairs."

Sydney's eyes cut to me before he left the house.

"Shall I ask the doctor to come up and see you?" Miss Pross asked.

"No, thank you," I said. "I'll be all right."

WHEN WE GOT behind the closed doors of Lucie's bedroom—or now, I supposed it was *our* bedroom—I hugged Charles tightly. It was weird that he and Sydney were almost as alike as identical twins but not related in any way. The only explanation for that in *A Tale of Two Cities* was that the two men bore an uncanny physical resemblance and that Sydney resented Charles because the other man reminded him of all he could have been but was not.

Putting that out of my mind, I said, "I'm sorry I let this happen. I shouldn't have walked away from him."

"It wasn't your fault. If anything, it was mine." He cupped my face in his hands. "I was on my way to ask him for a private word when one of the bankers took me aside and warned me not to be a 'Jerry sneak.' It took me a minute, but I understood that to mean a henpecked husband."

"Was it Mr. Lorry? Is he a silverfish?" I asked. "He was a good guy in the book, but now I'm thinking he's kind of a jerk."

"It wasn't Mr. Lorry but another of Tellson's employees. Mr. Lorry doesn't appear to be a silverfish, but as you'll recall from *Jane Eyre*, the characters in this Literatia-transformation of the book aren't always the same as they were in the original manuscript."

I remembered that well. Still, it didn't help matters at the moment. "I wonder if the banker distracted you on purpose to keep you away from Dr. Manette."

"He might've done so if he were a silverfish: but unless he's in league with the killer, I don't think his delaying me from speaking with Dr. Manette was to make sure the murder was carried out."

"Then who? Miss Pross? Isn't she rather frail to be heaving a heavy pot like that? Plus, Dr. Manette is quite a bit taller than she is. Miss Pross would have had to lift the pot way above her head in order to hit him." I sighed. "I should never have left him."

Charles gave me a comforting kiss on the forehead. "I

don't think you grasp yet how powerful the silverfish are. Once they've infiltrated a book, they're almost impossible to eradicate. Remember in *Jane Eyre* even after we'd apprehended the criminal, the silverfish continued to cling to their version of the story until they were finally forced to let go and allow the book to reset?"

"I do remember."

"Dr. Manette was going to die. Had one of us been his bodyguard the entire day and night, someone would have killed him in his sleep."

We heard footsteps on the stairs and quickly moved to the bed. I lay down, and Charles sat by my side with my hand in his.

There was a tap on the door before the man who'd pronounced Dr. Manette dead came into the room. "What a blow you have suffered, young lady, and on your wedding day no less."

"Did they find my father's assailant?" I asked, knowing full well they had not.

"I'm afraid they have not, but the constable is here now. He will make sure everything is put right." He dug around in his bag until he produced a small brown glass bottle. "I am leaving this tincture for you." He looked at Charles. "Make sure she takes it every two or three hours until the shock wears off."

"Of course," Charles said.

My eyes widened as I looked at Charles. He pressed my hand.

"Now, I must return to the salon. The undertaker is here."

Charles released my hand and stood. "I'll go with you."

"Nonsense." The doctor gave us a kind smile—no sign of silverfish. "There are plenty of able-bodied gentlemen in the house should we need them, and you should stay with your bride."

Once the doctor had left the room, I sat up. "The only person I know for sure didn't murder Dr. Manette was the Blackbird. I mean, that's what she reminded me of in looks and demeanor, but I was talking with her when Miss Pross screamed."

"The only person I can say for certain didn't commit the crime is the banker with whom I was speaking. From the corner of my eye, I saw Dr. Manette head for the kitchen. I tried to follow, but the man grasped my arm and said he'd like to hear my thoughts on the situation in France." He sat beside me on the bed.

"The banker purposefully detained you—twice. That looks mighty suspicious to me," I said. "His role might've been to keep you occupied so the killer could get Dr. Manette alone."

"That's possible, but he could merely be an old man who'd already had too much wine and enjoyed talking. How could anyone have guessed Dr. Manette would be alone in the kitchen at that particular time with all the activity in the house? There were guests and staff all over the house."

"True. It would have been challenging, to say the least, but I think it could have been done if someone had watched and waited with the patience of a spider." I gave an involuntary shudder.

Putting an arm around my shoulders, Charles said, "I don't think someone came in from outside. That's too random...unless, of course, an accomplice was waiting for a signal from someone inside the house."

"No, I agree. I feel the door was left open when the attacker made his or her escape. Unless that was a ruse to convince us the attacker was no longer in the house." I nestled my face against his broad chest. "I'm glad you're here. Living in the world of *Jane Eyre* was scary, but this novel is much more so. In *Jane Eyre*, we knew there was only one killer. In this book, it seems almost everyone is capable of murder to suit his or her own agenda."

CHAPTER 4

The next morning, I was dressed in my black mourning clothes and was putting white roses left over from the wedding into a vase. Charles had gone to make arrangements for Dr. Manette's funeral.

Last night, we'd slept together in our bed. Charles had offered to sleep on the floor, but I wouldn't hear of it. We were adults, and there was no reason we couldn't both sleep comfortably in the bed.

Don't get judgy on me, Reader. You wouldn't have wanted to sleep alone in that creepy house full of murderers and silver-fish either. Besides, other than our shoes and my infernal corset, we slept fully dressed.

When I awoke this morning, I was snuggled against Charles' right side. He was lying on his back, and I had hold of his arm. My face was pressed to his shoulder. It was wonderful.

He'd opened his eyes, turned his head, and smiled at

me. "Hi."

"Hey, there."

"Did you sleep well?" he asked.

"I did. I thought I'd be listening for intruders all night long, but my exhaustion must've gotten the better of me. How'd you sleep?"

"Fine."

"What's it like for you?" I ran a fingertip up and down his muscular forearm. "Jumping from one book to another all the time?"

"Shall I lie and tell you I'm used to it?" He chuckled softly. "You know what it's like when you travel from our world into this one. It's like that for me, except I'm almost constantly going from one book to another and have to figure out what book I'm in, what character I am, and what I'm doing there."

Groaning, I said, "I can't imagine how difficult that must be. At least, I have Cooper and Josephine giving me some intel before I go through the portal. You're always flying blind, aren't you? And you haven't been home in so long." I lowered my eyes. "It's time for that to change."

"From your lips to God's ear."

There'd come a knock then, and a maid had asked from the other side of the door if we wanted tea. We'd called to her that we'd be down for breakfast shortly and would have our tea then. Charles had gone into the guest room where his clothes were to change, and I'd put on a black dress I'd found in the closet.

Now here I was arranging roses like this was simply a

normal day in 1780. I couldn't imagine how difficult it must be for Charles. Had he been without electricity for forty years? I mean, of course, not seeing his son was the worst part. But the electricity—that had to be up near the top of the list.

Miss Pross came into the salon. "There's a nice couple here from France wishing to express their condolences about your father."

A chill trickled down my spine. "What are their names?"

"Monsieur and Madame Defarge."

I gripped the side of the table and took a steadying breath. Miss Pross rushed forward to place a hand on my arm, and I flinched.

"Poor dear," she murmured. "If you're unable to take visitors, I'll—"

"No, it's all right. See them in." I had to know why they were here and what they were up to.

Not trusting my knees to withstand the shock of seeing the Dafarges in the flesh, I hurried over to sit on the mahogany sofa.

Reader, that little sofa was no way near as comfy as the oversized leather couches in the Smithmore Manor library. There was a reason antique furniture looked as if it should be in a dollhouse or a museum—it should!

When Miss Pross ushered Monsieur and Madame Defarge into the room, I barely kept myself from wincing. They didn't look repulsive or threatening, but I remembered their characters—especially hers—too well from *A Tale of Two Cities* to realize I had to be particularly cautious around these two. In the original novel, they wanted Charles—and Lucie and their children—dead.

As Miss Pross left the room, Madame Defarge came to sit by my side and took my left hand in both of hers. I resisted the urge to tug my hand away.

"We are sorry for your loss." Her hand felt slightly damp on mine. "It must be such a shock."

"It is." I glanced at Monsieur Defarge as he took a seat on the chair opposite the sofa. "I've barely had time to process what happened."

"I imagine so," Monsieur Defarge said. "We're in London visiting a relative, and we came as soon as we heard the news."

Raising my brows, I said, "I didn't realize news traveled so quickly."

"Indeed, you *would* be surprised." He smiled at me, and I shivered as a silverfish wove through his bicuspids.

Dang it, Reader! These Defarges were bad enough without being silverfish too!

"You must be frightened," Madame Defarge said.

More than she could probably imagine, but I tried not to show it. "I'm more saddened than anything—and horrified that someone would kill my father in his own home with guests in the other room. I mean, how could such a thing happen?"

"How indeed?" Monsieur Defarge asked. "Your father —had he slipped back into the hopeless mental state he was in when you found him in my garret?"

When Lucie and Mr. Lorry had found Dr. Manette living in Monsieur Defarge's attic near the beginning of *A Tale of Two Cities*, the poor man did nothing but cobble shoes. He'd started the hobby while he was in prison.

And why was he in prison, Reader? Because he knew too much about the crimes of the Evremondes—one of whom was Charles Darnay's father. Dr. Manette didn't know Charles was an Evremonde—albeit renounced—until just prior to the wedding. What a mess, right?

Lifting my chin to defend the man I'd met only before he'd walked me down the aisle of the church, I said, "He had not. He was doing extremely well."

Sydney burst into the study. "I apologize for the interruption, but I believe Miss Manette needs her rest. As you know, she's suffered a terrible shock."

"Of course," Madame Defarge said. "We were getting ready to leave."

"Thank you, Mr. Carton," I said.

Monsieur Defarge narrowed his eyes at Sydney. "We merely wanted to see if there was anything we could do for *Mrs. Darnay*."

Sydney's jaw clenched. "The maid will see you out."

"Thank you for stopping by, Monsieur and Madame Defarge," I said. "I appreciate your concern."

"What did they want?" Sydney asked when the Defarges had left the room.

"They wished to express their condolences."

"I don't trust those two. I've heard rumors about their radical ideas."

"Tell me about it."

Reader, I hadn't meant for him to take me literally. I guess no one used that phrase sarcastically in the 1780s.

"They despise the aristocracy," he said. "They believe that if the Americans can break the chains of England, then the reformers can do the same here in France."

"How can one argue with that?" I asked. "Why wouldn't the French want their independence?"

"That's not the issue. Madame Defarge, in particular, despises the Evremondes and everyone associated with that family. They believe all aristocrats are bad and must pay for their misdeeds with their lives." When I didn't react, he added, "You're a part of the Evremonde family now."

Thankfully, Charles returned and saved me from having to converse on the subject anymore. I didn't like to discuss politics in the real world; I certainly didn't want to take on the topic in Literatia with a man who may or may not be a silverfish spying to see what he could learn about me and my intention to foil the destruction of *A Tale of Two Cities*.

"I feel unwell, Charles." I stood. "Would you take me upstairs?"

"Of course." He nodded to Sydney. "If you'll excuse us."

Piercing Charles with a stony gaze, Sydney said, "You shouldn't have abandoned your wife, Darnay."

"I didn't abandon her. I went to make the arrangements for her father's interment."

"Someone else could have done that." Sydney took my hand and raised it to his lips. "I'm here if you need anything."

"Thank you." When we were near the top of the stairs, I whispered to Charles, "I don't know what to make of him."

"As you know, it's best not to take anyone at face value."

When we got into our room, I opened the wardrobe to see if there was a panel that led to a hidden hallway. I hadn't thought to do that yesterday.

"I've already checked," Charles said. "There aren't any secret passages or hidden hallways in this house that the silverfish could use to spy on or attack us. The Manettes aren't quite as affluent as Edward Rochester was."

"Monsieur Defarge is a silverfish. Do you think Madame Defarge is too?" I asked. "She never really smiled."

Shaking his head slightly, he said, "Since Monsieur Defarge is a silverfish, I doubt she is one. The Silverfish Council wouldn't normally use their resources that extravagantly. If one member of the couple is a silverfish, there would be no need for the other to be." He blew out a breath. "That said, both the Defarges are dangerous. They were duplicitous in *A Tale of Two Cities*. Even if Mrs. Defarge pretends to be friendly here, we can't be sure she is."

"I'm almost positive she isn't." I took a seat on the edge of the bed. "It's awfully convenient that they were in

London visiting relatives when Dr. Manette was killed, don't you think?"

"Awfully." He sat beside me and then lay back on the bed so that he was looking up at the ceiling.

"They'd have needed help from someone inside the house, but they could very well be our killers," I said." Do you have any idea about any other silverfish who may be in the house?"

"Miss Pross."

My jaw dropped, and Charles nodded.

"I meant to warn you earlier not to take the woman into your confidence." He sat up.

"Are you sure?"

"Yep. She seldom smiles, but she did so just enough this morning that I caught a glimpse of a silverfish."

"What about Sydney?" I asked. "He doesn't smile either."

"I haven't seen any evidence that Sydney is a silverfish, but I don't trust the man."

"I don't trust anyone but you."

"And I don't trust anyone but you." He put an arm around my shoulders and kissed my temple.

"I'm glad you're here." I clung to him. "You make me feel safe."

But I'd have felt a lot safer were we not surrounded by silverfish and Defarges.

CHAPTER 5

Charles and I were having some tea, bread, and cheese in the salon. I'd have said we were having lunch, but lunch wasn't a thing yet. People in the 18th Century ate at weird times of the day, and book characters influenced by silverfish probably deviated even farther from the norm.

Generally, Reader, when I saw a piece of fruit or bread, I ate it because I didn't know when or if I'd get another chance.

Since we had no idea who might be listening, Charles and I had to be careful with what we said.

"I'm sorry I was out when Monsieur and Madame Defarge called on you," he said. "After we eat, I'm going to Tellson's to see if Mr. Lorry has an address for their relatives."

In other words, he was going to follow up to see if the Defarges were telling the truth. "May I go with you? I'd like to get some fresh air." Translation: I didn't want to stay here without him.

"Of course."

In *A Tale of Two Cities,* Charles Dickens describes Tellson's Bank as "very small, very dark, very ugly, very incommodious."

Reader, I couldn't paint you a better picture of the place than that, but I would add that it was gray...very gray.

As we walked down the street toward the bank, I held a handkerchief over my nose and mouth. The—ahem—toilet smells were almost unbearable. At least, they were to me. Most everyone else strolled along as if they were accustomed to it. Charles included.

When we entered the bank, we were able to close the door on the bathroom scents and enter the world of tobacco smoke and musty bank notes.

"Good afternoon!" Mr. Lorry was in the lobby and hurried over to greet us. "I trust the arrangements for Dr. Manette have been made?"

"Yes. The service will take place this evening," Charles said. "While I was out, Monsieur and Madame Defarge came to visit. I'd like to go by the house of the relative with whom they're staying and express my thanks for their consideration. Do you have a name or an address?"

"I'm sure I have something in my office. Follow me."

Charles gestured for me to walk ahead of him, and we trailed along behind Mr. Lorry, who chattered about the Defarges the whole way.

"—good people, terribly fond of Dr. Manette, you know. I imagine they were devastated when they heard the news." He ushered us inside the office, strode across the room, and threw open the doors of a cabinet. Inside were stacks of papers. How he ever found anything in there was beyond me. "Defarge...Defarge..."

I glanced around the office. It wasn't very decorative, with the exception of Mr. Lorry's ornately carved walnut desk. The top was mostly covered in papers, but I could see what looked like sunflowers at the corners and scrollwork along the sides. "Your desk is beautiful."

"Thank you, dear." Mr. Lorry turned with a look of mild puzzlement on his face. "You've seen it many times."

"Yes, I just—" I shrugged. "I don't believe I'd mentioned to you how much I admire it."

Mr. Lorry nodded, stepped closer to Charles, and lowered his voice. "You're giving her the tincture the doctor provided, aren't you?"

"Whenever she needs it. About that address?"

"Yes, yes." He glanced down at a sheet of paper he'd taken from the chest. "The Defarges' relative here in London is Samuel Appleby." He rattled off an address before returning the paper to the cabinet and closing the doors.

"We appreciate your help, Mr. Lorry," Charles said.

"Happy to oblige." Mr. Lorry extracted his pocket watch from his waistcoat pocket. "It's getting rather late in the day. Have you had the funeral cards prepared?"

"I have not. Under the circumstances, Lucie and I prefer to keep the affair private with only ourselves, you, and Miss Pross in attendance."

Mr. Lorry drew back as if Charles had slapped him. "Miss Pross will be there?"

"Why wouldn't she be? She has been with the Manettes since Lucie was a child."

Sniffing, Mr. Lorry said, "I believe Miss Pross knows more about Dr. Manette's murder than she has told us. Although she discovered the body and sounded the alarm, the miscreant was never found. One might assume Miss Pross allowed him time to abscond."

"What reason would Miss Pross have for wanting my father's killer to go free?" I realized *this* Miss Pross was a silverfish and that Mr. Lorry might very well be correct in his assumption, but the Miss Pross in the original novel was a fighter who took on—and ultimately killed— Madame Defarge in her defense of Lucie Manette.

"Perhaps she was frightened for her own safety, or perhaps she was an accomplice. One never truly knows what might be lurking in the mind of another." He narrowed his eyes at me. "Do you deny there are dark regions hidden in your own heart, Mrs. Darnay?"

What was he getting at? Before I could come up with a way to form the question as if I hadn't stepped through a portal into the 1700s yesterday, he spoke again.

"I cannot deny the darkness within me."

Was that a *threat*? Or a veiled confession?

"This conversation is distressing my wife." Charles gently took my arm. "I trust we'll see you at the funeral this evening?"

"Of course." Mr. Lorry followed us from his office. "Give my regards to Monsieur and Madame Defarge."

As soon as we were outside the bank, I asked Charles, "What did you make of that *darkness* garbage? Was he accusing me of something? Threatening? Confessing?"

"I have no idea. He was certainly eager to place blame on Miss Pross."

"Yeah, he was." I raised my handkerchief to cover my nose and mouth and didn't speak again. I decided anything else I had to say could wait until we were clear of the stench.

THE RELATIVE OF Monsieur and Madame Defarge wasn't a character in Dickens' original novel, so I was eager to meet Samuel Appleby. Was he a character from another book? Or was he merely an "extra" provided by the silverfish to accommodate this new plot development?

Upon arriving at the house, we were greeted by a butler and shown into the parlor of a nice country home to await Mr. Appleby. We didn't have to linger long before we were joined by a man of average height and weight. The man's wavy brown hair had been tied back into what had once been a tidy ponytail but was now coming apart. He wore a riding habit, and his face was flushed. We stood up from the sofa where we'd been sitting as he entered the room.

"I'm sorry to keep you waiting," he said. "I've just come in from a ride. Did John offer you tea?"

"We're fine," Charles said.

"Nonsense." The man strode to a side table and rang a bell. "Now then. I'm Samuel Appleby." He shook hands with Charles.

"Charles Darnay. And this is my wife, Lucie."

"A pleasure, madam." Mr. Appleby raised my gloved hand to his lips before turning back to Charles. "How may I be of service?" He gestured for us to resume our seats, and he sat on the chair adjacent to the sofa.

"We understand you're a relative of Monsieur Defarge and that he and his wife are visiting you at the moment," Charles said. "They called at our home this morning to pay their respects over the loss of Lucie's father, and I was out. I wanted to see them and express my gratitude for their thoughtfulness."

Reader, Charles had this 18th Century manners business down to a science. I was impressed.

"Ah, yes," Mr. Appleby said. "I apologize. They aren't here at the moment, but they mentioned Dr. Manette's passing. I'm terribly sorry for your loss, Mrs. Darnay."

"Thank you. Did you know my father?"

"No, but my cousin and his wife speak highly of him. They were ever so distraught at the news of his death."

John, the butler, brought in a tea service and poured us each a cup of the steaming black beverage. A delicate, sweet scent rose from the cups.

As John left, Charles picked the conversation up from where Mr. Appleby had left off.

"Were Monsieur and Madame Defarge here when they received the news of Dr. Manette's death?" he asked.

"No. They'd gone to speak with a vintner my cousin is considering partnering with. Ernest believes that he and this other wine merchant could corner the market in both London and Paris if they were to join forces."

"A *tranche* of two cities?" I chuckled. "Get it?"

Mr. Appleby frowned slightly but said, "Yes, exactly."

"Do you expect them back soon?" Charles asked.

"I've no idea. They left while I was out riding." He lifted his teacup to his lips.

"Was it the vintner who told them of Dr. Manette's demise?" Charles asked.

"It must have been because they knew of it when they returned yesterday."

Before Mr. Appleby could elaborate, Monsieur and Madame Defarge strolled into the parlor.

"The butler told us you were entertaining the Darnays, Samuel," Monsieur Defarge said.

"Yes." Charles stood and shook hands with Ernest Defarge. "I wanted to express to you and Madame Defarge my appreciation for your kindness to my wife earlier today and to her father years ago in his time of need."

"It was our pleasure." Monsieur Defarge smiled, and I lowered my eyes, not wanting to see the silverfish in his teeth.

"Dr. Manette was a good man." Madame Defarge squinted. "But that Mr. Carton—he bears watching."

"Did Mr. Carton do or say anything untoward to either of you while you were guests in our home?" Charles asked.

"He only suggested we take our leave." Monsieur Defarge pinned me with a suspicious glare. "Mr. Carton acted as if *he* were the man of the house."

Feeling put on the spot, I said, "Charles and I have known Mr. Carton for years, and he sometimes takes on the role of the overprotective older brother."

Monsieur Defarge's gaze slid from me to Charles as he muttered, "His affect didn't seem fraternal to me."

"Thank you for bringing Mr. Carton's behavior to my attention," Charles said. "I'll speak with him about it."

"Oh, we wouldn't want to cause anyone any trouble," Madame Defarge said.

The smirk on her lips and the malice in her eyes suggested quite the opposite—this woman had a keen desire to see heads roll. Literally.

CHAPTER 6

Charles and I walked behind the preacher, who followed the men carrying the coffin. The rest of the mourners plodded after Charles and me. Despite our telling Mr. Lorry we wanted the procession to be a family affair, we were joined by Mr. Stryver (the lawyer), Miss Pross, Mr. Lorry, Mr. Carton, the Defarges, and Mr. Appleby. I supposed Mr. Appleby felt obliged to pay his respects after we'd visited him earlier in the day.

At the cemetery, the grave was already dug. I swallowed a lump in my throat as my eyes welled. I knew deep down this man was a fictional character, but he'd walked me down the aisle to my groom less than forty-eight hours ago.

The preacher said a few words about what a kind and noble man Dr. Manette had been and commended his soul into the care of our Lord. After that, the box was lowered into the ground.

Charles tucked my hand into the bend of his elbow and led me from the churchyard. The funeral cortege followed us home.

Reader, this was beginning to feel like the longest night of my life.

At the Manette home, a light supper had been prepared by the cook. Most of the guests served themselves; but rather than have something to eat, Madame Defarge sat on a chair and took her knitting from a deep pocket in her skirt.

I strolled over to her chair and watched the knitting needles dart through the yarn. "You do lovely work. What are you making?"

"It's a tapestry." She didn't look up at me. "I'm using it to note important events."

Noticing an intricate *A* followed by *Mane*, I asked, "Are you knitting my father's name into your tapestry?" Because it looked as if it could very well be *Alexandre Manette* she intended to write.

The needles stopped clicking momentarily, and Madame Defarge glanced up at me. "Yes. Your father deserves to be remembered."

"Thank you." Before walking away, I thought I saw the word *Traitor* above my father's name. I knew not to believe anything Madame Defarge said, but that word was a harsh statement of how quickly she was ready to condemn my father. And for what? For letting his daughter marry an aristocrat? A *former* aristocrat?

I looked for Charles but saw that he was in conversation with Mr. Stryver and Mr. Lorry, so I wandered over to the fireplace. As I regarded the flames leaping in the grate, I wondered if Madame Defarge really was designating Dr. Manette a traitor or if she'd applied that label to someone else.

"Did the Defarge woman say something to upset you?"

I started at the sound of Sydney's voice, finding it a bit unnerving that he watched me as closely as he did. "No. She said my father deserved to be remembered."

"I don't trust the Defarges," he said.

"I know. You've made that clear."

"What can I say? I feel protective of you."

"I appreciate your concern," I said, "but I'm quite capable of looking out for myself."

Before Sydney could respond, Charles joined us. "Thank you, Carton, for keeping my wife company. I feel it's time we should bid our guests goodnight and retire." He inclined his head toward me. "My poor darling is exhausted."

"Very well." Sydney's eyes cut from Charles to me. "Goodnight."

After Sydney left, Charles announced to the room that he was grateful for their condolences but that he felt it was time they all got some sleep. The guests filed by us and expressed their sympathies again.

When at last they'd all gone, Charles and I climbed the stairs, went to our room, and took off our shoes. This time I stripped down to the four layers of clothing that were beneath my mourning gown.

"I'll have to wear that again tomorrow, and I don't want it to be wrinkled," I said.

"Good thinking." Charles removed his jacket and waistcoat and hung them on the bedpost.

Once we were under the covers, I told Charles about Madame Defarge's tapestry. "She was adding Dr. Manette's name to it, and above his name, I saw the word *traitor*. I don't know if she was labeling him as such or not."

Of course, we were both well aware that Madame Defarge's knitting in *A Tale of Two Cities* was a registry of those the woman felt should face the guillotine.

"It's likely she did label Dr. Manette a traitor because he welcomed me into his family." Charles adjusted the pillow beneath his head. "To the Defarges' way of thinking, when Dr. Manette learned I was an Evremonde before renouncing my family name, he should have refused to allow me to marry you."

"But you *did* reject the Evremonde name and took on an anglicized version of your mother's maiden name, D'Aulnais. You turned your back on the aristocracy."

"True, but it would have been perfectly understandable had Dr. Manette refused to allow the marriage to proceed. After all, Charles Evremonde's father was one of the men responsible for Dr. Manette's wrongful imprisonment."

"But he recognized that Charles was not his father and was, in fact, a good and honorable man."

Charles reached out and caressed my face. "Still, in the original manuscript, he had a nine-day mental break after the wedding."

"When you came into this book, were you Charles Evremonde or Charles Darnay?" I asked. "What happened when you were pulled from *Jane Eyre*? Was it my fault you weren't able to come home with me?"

"No, not in the least. I'd have thought Cooper would have explained why I haven't been out of Literatia in so long."

"He did, but I'm not sure I fully understand the situation."

"When the silverfish saw how easily Cooper could move back and forth between the two worlds when he was a child, they insisted as part of a peace treaty on keeping a member of the Wellingham family in Literatia at all times as insurance against Cooper one day coming to completely destroy them."

Raising up on my elbow, I asked, "Cooper could do that—wipe out the entire silverfish population?"

"I'm not sure. It's possible. Cooper has powers beyond those any of the other Wellinghams have ever had—as far as we know. For years, Cooper's mother and I took turns staying in Literatia."

I turned my gaze to the eyelet-edged sheet. "Wasn't that hard on your marriage?"

"Somewhere along the way, our relationship had

become less of a marriage and more of a partnership in parenting Cooper. We were companionable but no longer passionate toward each other. Keeping Cooper safe and guarding the books in Literatia became our focus."

Lifting my eyes to his once more, I said, "It's absurd that time passes so much more slowly here that Cooper seems older than you."

"I know. It's crazy. Plus, when his mother got sick, I took over all the duties of Literatia so they could be together before she died. I've missed so much time with him." Shaking off his melancholy, he asked, "Does it bother you that I'm such an old man? If it does—"

I interrupted him with a kiss to show him just how little his age bothered me.

THE NEXT MORNING, Miss Pross, Charles, and I were having breakfast together. I decided it was the perfect time to pump Miss Pross for information.

"Miss Pross, thank you so much for your dedication to our family," I said. "You've always been selfless." Best to butter her up before beginning my inquiry.

The old lady's lips spread slightly in a demure smile. Thankfully, no silverfish appeared. "You're ever so welcome, my dear. It has been my pleasure."

"Did you see or hear anything unusual the day my father died?" I spread jam onto my bread and didn't look up at her. "Even something of little consequence that might direct the constable to my father's assailant?"

"I've already told the constable everything I know," she said, her voice sounding reedy and defensive. "I didn't see anything or anyone."

"We know you gave a full account of your experience to the constable, Miss Pross," Charles said gently. "Or, at least, everything you felt was pertinent at the time. But emotions often cloud our thinking immediately after we go through something traumatic. I'm sure Lucie was simply wondering if, now that a little time has passed, you might recall something you'd previously forgotten to mention."

She shook her head vehemently. "No. Nothing at all."

"Did my father have any last words?" I asked.

"Yes, as a matter of fact, his last thoughts were of you. The last word he uttered was your name."

Even though I knew how duplicitous and conniving the silverfish were, I said, "Thank you, Miss Pross, for being a comfort to him as he drew his last breath." I watched the woman's weathered face for any flicker of guilt or regret, but there was none.

After we ate, I suggested Charles and I go for a stroll in the garden. As soon as he and I were alone, I heaved a sigh.

"How are we ever going to discover who killed Dr. Manette? Miss Pross is obviously lying. If she didn't murder him herself, then she had to have seen *something* that would lead us to the truth." I let out a growl of frustration. "I want to grab her and shake her! I know it wouldn't do any good and those nasty silverfish might come loose and crawl all over me, but I'm so aggravated!"

Charles put a comforting arm around my waist. "I know, darling. It vexes me too, but we'll have to be smarter than the silverfish."

"It just seems like it was easier to solve the mystery in *Jane Eyre*. We had a finite number of suspects, and everyone was gathered together at Thornfield Hall."

"You only *think* it was easier because that mystery has been solved. Did you really believe it was easy at the time?"

Resting my head against his shoulder, I said, "No. But what do we do now? We have no leads and no idea where to point the finger."

"When you're in Literatia and unsure of how to direct the narrative, you need only wait for the silverfish to tip their hand. What was the desire of the villains in *A Tale of Two Cities*?"

"The villains—in particular, Madame Defarge—wanted Charles Darnay and his family to face the guillotine."

"Exactly," Charles said. "The silverfish must accomplish this goal as soon as possible if they are to destroy the book."

I stopped walking and stared up at Charles. "How? Lucie and Charles' wedding was eight years before the storming of the Bastille. Are you telling me we have to wait *eight years* before we can solve Dr. Manette's murder and restore the manuscript to its original state?"

He smiled down at me. "No. They're certain they have the upper hand, so the silverfish will continue to consume the story until it's constantly mutating. The killer's motive will soon become apparent." He brushed a lock of hair out of my eyes. "Would it be so terrible if we *were* to remain here for eight years and have a family?"

"Would our children be real? Could we take them with us when we return home?"

Charles shook his head.

"Then, no, I couldn't bear it. Have you ever—?" I trailed off, unable to finish the sentence.

"Although I've been stuck in manuscripts for varying lengths of time, I have no offspring—no fictional ones anyway. You're acquainted with my only child."

"When you are stuck in a manuscript, what do you do?"

"I live someone else's life." He shrugged.

"That's horrible." I stepped closer and hugged him.

"It's not always so bad. Some characters have rich, adventurous lives, and others are sedate and studious. I've resigned myself to the fact that my life is what it is. I'm stuck here."

"You won't always be," I said. "I promise you that."

CHAPTER 7

After having decided it might be best to divide and conquer, Charles went to see Mr. Lorry the next day while I set my sights on learning something useful from Miss Pross. Finding her sitting in the salon by the window with an embroidery sampler on her lap, I sat across from her and asked how she was doing.

Looking slightly taken aback and suspicious of my concern—not sure whether that was due to her being a silverfish or a servant in the Manette household—she placed her needlework on the table next to her and folded her hands.

"I'm unsure of my feelings, dear, since there are so many of them constantly battling for precedence," she said. "I feel guilty for not being able to stop Dr. Manette's attack, sadness at his death, fear for you, resolve to be stalwart for this family…"

"I appreciate your wanting to be strong for Charles

and me, but don't forget you're a part of this family too. We must all lean on each other during this crisis." I then addressed the matter I'd sought out Miss Pross to discuss. "At the wedding reception, there was a woman here who reminded me of a blackbird."

The older woman stiffened.

"She was dressed all in black, even though she was at a wedding reception rather than a funeral, and she was small with beady eyes," I continued. "She was talking with me when I heard you scream—you'd found my father on the floor. I don't think I got the woman's name. Do you know who she might be?"

Quickly shaking her head, Miss Pross said, "No, no, I don't know anyone fitting that description. No one at all."

She was clearly lying, and it was apparent to me that Miss Pross was frightened of Blackbird. But why would she be? Cooper had mentioned to me once that there were both lesser silverfish and greater silverfish. I was guessing Blackbird outranked Miss Pross in the silverfish hierarchy.

"I don't suppose it matters." I shrugged. "I was merely curious. The blackbird must have attended the wedding with one of the other guests."

"Precisely." Miss Pross swallowed convulsively. "There's no reason for you to be concerned about this woman. I don't think she had anything to do with your father's attack."

Before I could speak with her further, we were interrupted by the maid.

"Mrs. Darnay, Mr. Carton is here to see you."

"Please show him in," I said.

He'd been right outside the salon door because when I asked the maid to show him in, Sydney strode into the room.

"I apologize for my forwardness, but I couldn't help overhearing your discussion of some suspicious woman," he said. "What's that all about?"

Forwardness indeed, Reader! Still, he might know something about Blackbird.

"There was a small woman all dressed in black at the wedding reception," I said. "I was speaking with her when my father was attacked."

The knuckles on Miss Pross's folded hands turned white because she was clasping them so tightly.

Sydney walked over to stand by the fireplace. "A small woman dressed all in black?"

"That's right. Neither Miss Pross nor I are acquainted with the woman and aren't sure why she was here. You wouldn't happen to know the woman, would you, Sydney?"

"I don't, but I'll certainly make some inquiries," he said.

Miss Pross stood. "If you'll excuse me, I need to go to my room and rest for a little while."

"Of course." I gave her what I hoped was a reassuring smile. "Please let me know if you need anything."

Once Miss Pross had gone, Sydney took the chair she'd vacated. He leaned forward, rested his forearms on his thighs, and spoke just above a whisper. "She's lying. She knows full well the woman you're describing. I can tell by her manner."

"I agree. I'm not only convinced that Miss Pross knows the woman but that she's frightened of her."

"Why do you think Miss Pross would be afraid of her?" he asked.

"I'm not sure." I had my suspicions but nothing I could share with Sydney Carton. "The woman must hold some sway over Miss Pross. I need to know who she is and what influence she might have over people in my household."

Sydney stood, stepped closer, and reached for my hand.

I extended my hand to him, and he raised it to his lips.

"I shall discover the identity of this woman and bring you all the information I can find as soon as possible. In the meantime, be on your guard," he said. "With everyone."

He strode from the room, and I walked over to the table where Miss Pross had left her needlework. Picking it up, I examined it closely to see if she was following in the footsteps of Madame Defarge and creating a registry of aristocrats who should die at the guillotine. As far as I could tell, it was an innocent, bucolic scene.

I WAS PACING the salon when Charles got home. "How did your meeting with Mr. Lorry go?"

"He swears he saw nothing and has no idea who'd have a grudge against Dr. Manette. Someone came to see Mr. Lorry while I was there. He was a burly man, and he was waiting outside Lorry's office when I left. The man barged into the office nearly before I could clear the door and demanded to know if Lorry had the money owed to his boss."

"That's interesting. Maybe we should check to see if Dr. Manette owed money to anyone," I said. "I asked Miss Pross about the woman who reminded me of a blackbird, and although she denied knowing the woman, she was frightened by my questions."

"Then this 'blackbird' must be the character designated by the silverfish council to oversee the destruction of the book."

"Sydney stopped by while I was questioning Miss Pross, and he's promised to learn all he can about the woman in black."

Clenching his jaw, Charles asked, "What was he doing here? It seems he lives here half the time."

"I know." I put my hand on his arm. "And that's not all. Before Dr. Manette was killed, Sydney asked me if I was having second thoughts about marrying you. He told me to say the word, and he'd have our union annulled."

"What did you tell him?" Charles asked.

"I said I was happy with you—that it was my father I was concerned about."

Charles stalked across the room to the window and looked outside. "That man is up to no good. I can feel it."

Joining him at the window, I said, "Don't forget that in *A Tale of Two Cities*, Charles Darnay wasn't overly fond of Sydney Carton, but Sydney saved his life."

"And don't *you* forget that this Sydney Carton is a mutation of the character he was in the original novel, and so far, he's given us every reason to be distrustful of him." He turned to face me. "He has a knack for coming here when I'm not home. I don't like his being here, and I don't want you to be lulled into trusting the man."

"I don't trust him in the least, but I'm eager to discover what he can find out about the blackbird."

After tapping on the door, the maid entered. "I have a letter for you, Mr. Darnay."

"Thank you." Charles met her in the middle of the room and took the envelope.

She left and closed the door as Charles crossed to the desk, took out a letter opener, and removed the note.

I was quiet for as long as I could be while he read. Finally, I asked, "What is it?"

"It's from Gabelle."

In *A Tale of Two Cities,* Gabelle was an employee of the Evremonde family who was wrongfully accused of treason. He begged Charles to come and save his life. Charles went and was immediately imprisoned for being a member of the French aristocracy.

"And so it begins," Charles said softly.

"No." I hurried over to him. "We're not ready. Plus, we don't have children. I mean, before Charles Darnay went to Paris in *A Tale of Two Cities*, he and Lucie had been married for eight years and had a son and daughter. This letter shouldn't be here yet."

Charles turned, put the letter aside, and cradled me against him. "The silverfish are constantly altering the manuscript. They're seeking to further their agenda."

"Neither of us are ready for a trip to Paris. It's too dangerous. Besides, Dr. Manette's murder took place *here*. His killer is here." I shut my eyes and tightened my arms around Charles' waist. "The silverfish are speeding up the timeline in order to keep us from solving Dr. Manette's murder."

"While that's likely true, I don't see that we have much say in the matter. We need the manuscript to continue moving forward whether that's by our design or by that of the silverfish. Otherwise, we're allowing them to win."

"But you said you've lived for years in some novels," I said, hoping my voice didn't sound as whiny to him as it did to my own ears.

"I have. But the silverfish didn't appear to have the sense of urgency they have with this book."

"So why is this one so important to them?"

"I believe it's because you solved the *Jane Eyre* mystery so quickly," he said, rubbing his hands up and down my back in a soothing manner.

"*We* solved that mystery together."

"Yes. We're a formidable team. The silverfish are desperate to prevent us from solving this mystery and snatching another beloved classic from them." He kissed the top of my head. "I must go to Paris and attempt to save Gabelle—while seeing what the silverfish have in store for me there."

Reader, I knew good and well what the silverfish had in store for him there—La Guillotine! And if Matthew were to die in Literatia as Charles Darnay, he would also be dead in our world. I wasn't about to let that happen.

"One day won't make much of a difference, will it?" I asked.

He held me at arm's length and looked down into my eyes. "What are you up to?"

"I'm thinking we need to buy ourselves some time. Perhaps you could take the letter to Mr. Lorry and ask him to verify that the letter is truly from Gabelle. Surely some of Mr. Lorry's contacts at Tellson's Bank in Paris can find that out."

"But making those inquiries will take much longer than a day."

I smiled. "Exactly. It will, hopefully, give us time to solve the murder. And, to the silverfish, it will simply seem you're being cautious."

"Excellent point. But instead of Mr. Lorry, I'll hire Mr. Stryver, the attorney, to check the veracity of the note. I'll say that following Dr. Manette's brutal murder, I'm afraid this note might be a ruse to persuade me to leave London and isolate my bride, making her vulnerable to attack. After all, Dr. Manette's killer hasn't been found, and my utmost priority must be to protect my wife."

"That's perfectly logical," I said. "Is Mr. Stryver a silverfish?"

"I don't think so, but this interaction will give me the opportunity to see what he knows and for us to control the advancement of the narrative for a while."

"I only hope it's long enough." With a shudder, I stepped back into the haven of Charles' arms.

CHAPTER 8

As it turned out, Charles didn't have to make a trip to Mr. Stryver's office. He came to us. The man who at one point in *A Tale of Two Cities* wanted to marry Lucie—not because he loved her but because he believed her beauty and virtuousness would help him professionally—strutted into the salon and eyed both Charles and me with ill-concealed disdain. Mr. Dickens had described the man as "stout, loud, and free from any drawback of delicacy." As far as I could tell, Mr. Stryver hadn't changed much from that original description. If anything, he was worse.

Charles and I were still standing in the center of the room when Stryver came into the salon, dropped onto the sofa, and put his feet up on the coffee table.

While it was out of character for Lucie Manette, I couldn't hold my tongue. "Mr. Stryver, our family isn't in the habit of using my late grandmother's table as a footstool, and I'd appreciate it if you didn't either."

Reader, who knew where that coffee table came from, other than the imagination of Charles Dickens? It could have belonged to Dr. Manette's mother. The fact remained that I wasn't about to let this boorish man come into the place I was pretending was my home and be disrespectful.

"Oh, ho, ho!" Stryver swung his feet to the floor and raised his thick eyebrows at Charles. "Better you than me, sir."

"Indeed," Charles said. "I'm glad you're here, Mr. Stryver—you've saved me a trip." He handed Stryver the letter from Gabelle. "I need this authenticated by some of your Parisian colleagues. I would, of course, be obliged to assist Gabelle if he has truly been incarcerated. However, receiving the letter so soon after Dr. Manette's murder, I'm afraid it could be a ruse."

Stryver took the letter, opened it, and briefly glanced at its contents before folding it and tucking it into the pocket of his waistcoat. "I'll have someone sort this out. But, for your information, I didn't take valuable time out of my day to merely pay you a social call, Darnay. I came here about the fee for Dr. Manette's will."

"What about it?" I asked.

Stryver acted as if I hadn't spoken a word and continued addressing my husband.

Such enlightened times!

"As I imagine you're aware, I prepared Dr. Manette's last will and testament. He had promised to pay my fee the day after the wedding. In light of the extenuating circumstances, I shall give you until the end of the week to make remuneration." He stood. "Good day."

I opened my mouth to protest his attempt to extort money out of us right after my pretend father's death, but I closed it again and gave Stryver a tight smile. I'd realized it was easy to get caught up in this world where Charles and I—not to mention the silverfish—were only actors playing a part. And Stryver might've just given us his motive for killing Dr. Manette. If he'd come to ask us to pay his fee so soon after the funeral, he was either extremely greedy or had to be hard up for money.

As soon as I was sure the man had left our house, I said as much to Charles.

"I was thinking the same thing," he said. "The next time our pal Carton drops in, I'll ask him about Stryver's financial situation." He took my hand. "Please don't think I'm only being jealous when I asked you to avoid Sydney Carton when I'm away from home. I have a bad feeling about that man."

"All right." I grinned. "It's fine with me, though, if you're a *little* jealous."

He pulled me closer. "Maybe I'm more than a little jealous, but don't let that go to your head."

"Never." I tilted my face up for a kiss.

Reader, wouldn't you know it? The maid interrupted us for the umpteenth time to tell us we had a visitor. But this time it was worth it—it was Vidocq!

Eugene Francois Vidocq was a brilliant criminal who

became known as the first private detective. I'd read Vidocq's memoir and then had become friends with him in the world of *Jane Eyre*. I hadn't dreamed I'd encounter Vidocq in the world of *A Tale of Two Cities* because he was much too young when the first part of the book took place.

When he strolled into the salon with that ever-present twinkle in his eyes, he was indeed at least forty years younger than he'd been at Thornfield Hall.

"Vidocq!" Laughing, I ran and threw myself into his waiting arms. "How can this be? How are you here?"

He joined in my laughter, then kissed me on both cheeks and shook hands with Charles. Then he and I sat on the sofa, and Charles took the chair across from us. Charles looked as bemused as I felt.

"You must forgive me, Edward Rochester," Vidocq said to Charles. "By appearing here as the younger, more handsome version of myself, I am likely to steal away the heart of sweet Gia."

"That's a possibility," Charles said. "Still, it's good to see you again, *mon ami*. By the way, here we are Lucie and Charles."

"*Oui*, of course, and I will address you as such if I must."

"I never thought I'd see you again." I blinked away the tears that sprang to my eyes. "How *are* you here?"

Sandwiching my hand between his, he said, "As I told you in the world of *Jane Eyre*, I exist always and everywhere in Literatia. It is because I have been written about extensively in both fiction and nonfiction." He smiled. "It is the nonfiction accounts—in particular, my own memoirs, which I believe you have read and enjoyed—that allow me to move about so unencumbered."

"I still don't quite understand how you're here; I'm just glad you are."

"You wonder *how* Vidocq is here, yet you fail to question *why*. Have I taught you nothing, *ma petite*?"

"Sorry. I was so delighted to see you that I never even considered putting on my proverbial detective hat."

"Nor did I," Charles admitted.

"Ah, but you both must be on your guard at all times." He let go of my hand to tap an index finger against his head. "Always be wearing the detective hats. Time passes quickly in the books of the original manuscript, and you can lose control of the narrative to the silverfish *tres vite* if you aren't careful. That is why Vidocq is here to help."

"Did Cooper send you?" Charles asked.

"This time, I was summoned by his associate, Josephine."

A worried frown crossed Charles's face, but he quickly hid it. "What exactly did she tell you?"

"Only that I must make haste to assist you because the silverfish are attempting to accelerate the execution of Charles Darnay." Vidocq's voice betrayed none of the gravity of our situation; but, of course, we knew. The death of Charles Darnay would mean not only the complete destruction of *A Tale of Two Cities*, but it would also result in the death of Matthew.

I went in search of the maid and told her to make up the guest room for Monsieur Vidocq, Charles' cousin who was visiting from France. She didn't question the fact that Vidocq had arrived with no luggage. Frankly, I didn't question it myself. Either he didn't expect to be here long enough to require much, or else a trunk would be delivered for him in a day or two. I still didn't fully understand how he was here, so much closer to my age than he'd been in *Jane Eyre*, and how his younger self knew people he'd met when he was much older. I was simply happy he was here. Certainly, with Vidocq's help, we could now solve the mystery of Dr. Manette's murder.

Over dinner, Vidocq regaled Charles and me with tales of duels he had fought, but Charles was unusually reserved. Was he concerned about Cooper? Or was it the fact that the silverfish seemed determined to end this story and/or his life?

I was torn. I wanted to speak with Charles alone and reassure him that all was well back at home and that we'd get out of this book so he could soon see for himself. But I also wanted a private word with Vidocq. I'd gotten to know him well enough during our time together at Thornfield Hall that I realized he was holding something back from us.

CHAPTER 9

Shortly after dinner, the maid arrived in the salon to say Vidocq's room was ready. He stood, bowed slightly to Charles and me, and said he was weary and wished to go on to bed.

"I'll show you to your room," I said quickly.

He bestowed a smile on me that was second only to the Mona Lisa in its inscrutability. "I do not wish to trouble you. I'm sure the maid will provide me with adequate direction."

"I insist." I was speaking through gritted teeth but trying to sound gracious. "What sort of hostess would I be if I failed to show our esteemed guest to his room?"

"Very well." He left the room and headed for the stairs.

I hurried to match his strides. "What aren't you telling us?"

"I am not telling you that you are even more

enchanting as Lucie Manette Darnay than you were as Jane Eyre because I would venture to say that Gia outshines both women."

"I'd thank you if I didn't think you were merely using that silver tongue to avoid my question," I said. "There's something serious going on—I know it."

"*Mais oui*. It is ever so important that the silverfish are attempting to destroy this beloved classic and kill Charles Darnay. We must stop them."

Reader, I knew there was more to it than that. I kept pressing him for answers, and he kept denying he was keeping anything from me.

When we reached his room, he said, "This is where we must say *bonne nuit*, Madame Darnay—unless, of course, there is something more you wish to do to make me feel more welcome." He waggled his bushy eyebrows at me as he removed his coat.

A folded-over piece of paper fell from one of the inside pockets onto the floor. Vidocq attempted to step on the note, but I kicked it away from his foot and then snatched it up.

Unfolding the paper, my eyes went immediately to the signature. The note was from Josephine. I started at the top and read the entire note then.

Josephine thought Cooper had suffered a stroke. He'd been fatigued and achy earlier in the morning, and she'd hoped he only had a cold or some sort of viral infection. But when she had gone up to check on him, the right side of his face was drooping. She told Vidocq

G. LEESON

she hadn't allowed me to see him because she was afraid I'd alarm Matthew. Cooper insisted the mission was critical and had asked her to send Vidocq to help us.

I looked from the letter to Vidocq, my eyes filling as I tried to swallow the lump in my throat. My voice emerged as a whisper. "What are we going to do?"

He stepped forward and put his hands on my shoulders. "We are going to solve this mystery as soon as possible."

Holding up the note, I asked, "Why didn't Josephine burn this on her side? When I was first transported into *Jane Eyre*, Cooper spoke to me through a note in my reticule, and he burned it. It turned to ash right before my eyes."

"Josephine is not as experienced as Cooper."

"I've got to get Matthew back home, Vidocq. Will you help me?"

"*Bien sur!* Of course!"

"We should burn this paper before the silverfish see it," I said. "Don't you think?"

"Probably. I'll take care of it." He took the paper from me. "And Matthew—er, Charles. What will you tell him?"

"I have no idea."

I WENT to the room I shared with Charles to find that he was already there.

"Did you get what you wanted?" he asked, a grin playing about his lips.

"And what would that be?"

"To find out what Vidocq is keeping from us."

Laughing, I said, "How do you know me so well?"

He shrugged. "So, did Vidocq open up to you?"

"No, but there had to be a good reason Cooper thought it was imperative to send him to assist us. Think about it—if the Defarges were somehow able to send both of us to the guillotine, then who would there be, other than Cooper, to protect Literatia?"

"That's an excellent point, but I'm still concerned that Vidocq knows more than he's letting on."

"I agree, but there's no doubt he's on our side and will eventually tell us what we need to know. Right?"

Charles nodded. "I suppose you're right."

Reader, I felt a hundred and fifty levels of guilty for not divulging to Charles everything I knew. But his concern over Cooper would be a hindrance rather than a help at this point. Otherwise, Vidocq would have told us immediately. I absolutely had to make certain that if this time only one of us could escape the book, it would be Charles.

SYDNEY CARTON ARRIVED the next morning while Charles, Vidocq, and I were in the salon going over the events surrounding Dr. Manette's death. The maid announced Sydney's arrival, and we'd changed the subject of our discussion to Vidocq's journey to England by the time she ushered Sydney into the room.

"Ah, Mr. Carton, I'd like you to meet my cousin, Eugene Francois Vidocq," Charles said.

Vidocq, who was sitting beside me on the sofa rose to shake Sydney's hand.

Sydney, eyes narrowed as they traveled between Vidocq and me, shook the other man's hand. "You are from France?"

"*Oui.*" Vidocq gave Sydney a tight smile. "How did you become acquainted with my kinsman and his beautiful bride, *monsieur?*"

"I've been friends with them since I helped defend Charles when he was falsely accused of treason several years ago," Sydney said, taking a seat on the chair adjacent to the one in which Charles sat. "The only evidence against your cousin was the testimony of an eyewitness. When I pointed out the physical resemblance between Charles and me and, thus, the fallibility of the witness's testimony, the prosecution's case fell apart."

"*Bravo.*" Vidocq inclined his head. "I suppose you and Charles do bear a passing resemblance." Winking at me, he added, "See that you do not get confused, *ma belle.*"

Sydney turned to Charles. "You are all right with your cousin's forward manner with your wife?"

"I assure you it's harmless," Charles said with a smile. "Vidocq has always been a favorite of the ladies, and he knows it." Before Sydney could say anything further, he added, "Do you have any news to share about our mystery wedding guest?"

"It was hard to pin down any solid information about her," Sydney said. "No one seemed to know for certain who she attended the wedding with, but she is a known associate of Ernest and Therese Defarge. In addition, she has ties to a lawyer in America."

"We still don't know how she knew Dr. Manette or what exactly she was doing here," Charles said.

"My best guess, given her affiliation with the Defarges, is that she'd perhaps met Dr. Manette while he was staying in their garret," Sydney said.

Shaking my head, I said, "That makes no sense. My father wasn't in his right mind while he was staying in that garret. He didn't recover until Mr. Lorry and I brought him back home to England."

"Tell us more about these ties to an American lawyer," Vidocq said. "Is she related to this person, or does she have business dealings with him?"

"I don't know." Sydney shifted in his seat. "I got the impression that the woman—referred to as Madame Grievous—moves in some powerful circles."

The maid interrupted to tell us that Mr. Lorry had arrived and needed to speak with Charles privately.

"Please show Mr. Lorry to my study." Charles rose. "Excuse me, I'll be back as quickly as I can."

After Charles had left the room, I turned to Vidocq. "What do you think this Madame Grievous is doing here?"

My questioning Vidocq obviously upset Sydney.

"What are you asking *him* for?" he asked. "I'm the one who brought you the information about her."

I scrambled to appease him. "Yes, and I'm grateful to you for doing so. I was actually addressing you both, as Monsieur Vidocq has a great many allies both here and in France. I thought he'd perhaps heard of her before."

"I have a great many enemies, too, *ma petite*," Vidocq said. "Never forget that."

I smiled. "It's because you are incorrigible." He'd told me once at Thornfield Hall that had we met in his youth, I might have made him *corrigible*. I believed that to be an impossibility and that Vidocq was born to be incorrigible, but it was a nice memory.

He, too, must've remembered our joke because he laughed and patted my hand. "Is it too late, do you think?"

"Always. Now back to my question—do either of you gentlemen have a theory as to what Madame Grievous is doing here?"

"Working with the Defarges, of course," Vidocq said. "Monsieur Carton, are you aware that my cousin is by birth a member of French aristocracy? And that Monsieur and Madame Defarge wish to wipe out every nobleman and his family?"

"I'm aware," Sydney said. "But despite Charles being of noble birth, Lucie isn't. She's not even French, and they haven't been married long enough for anyone to consider Lucie a member of the aristocracy." He stood and began to pace.

"It was you who warned me about the Defarges," I reminded Sydney. "You know how heavily they're involved in the revolt."

He came to sit on the other side of me. "The Defarges are indeed dangerous radicals, but this need not concern you. You are not French nobility—they can't harm you."

"They can, and they will," Vidocq said. "Furthermore, if Lucie carries a child, that child is a French aristocrat."

Sydney sprang to his feet. "How dare you speak of such delicate matters before Miss Manette?"

"I speak the truth to Mrs. Darnay because she deserves to know it." Vidocq slowly rose, his hands clenching into fists at his sides.

I got up and moved between them before they came to blows. "Please, gentlemen." To Sydney, I said, "Monsieur Vidocq is correct. Charles was born into the French aristocracy. Even though he denounced it and anglicized his name because he didn't approve of his family's actions, his blood is that of a nobleman. As his wife, I can also be bprove an aristocrat in the eyes of people like the Defarges and, I imagine, Madame Grievous."

Sydney stepped closer to me. "I won't let anyone hurt you. I swear it."

"And how will you protect her, *monsieur*?" Vidocq asked.

"By making sure the Defarges and their cronies get nowhere near her while they're in England and—" He looked from Vidocq to me. "You must never, under any circumstances, go to France, Lucie. At least, not until this madness is over." He grasped my hands. "Promise me."

Vidocq took me firmly by the waist and propelled me backward before stepping in front of me and disengaging my hands from Sydney's. "Monsieur Carton, you admonished me for being too forward with my cousin's wife, and yet your own actions are an insult to them both! I am willing to believe you were merely overcome by fear for the Darnays' safety and unable to control your actions. However, you will apologize to Mrs. Darnay at once."

"My familiarity? You put your hands on her *waist!*"

"I did only what was necessary to remove my kinsman's bride from the clutches of a rake," Vidocq said. "I've heard no apology from you yet. Shall we duel?"

"Vidocq, no!" I cried.

After taking a deep breath, he said, "Perhaps you are correct in thinking me too rash, *madame*. I humbly apologize for causing you undue alarm."

"As do I," Sydney said. "I would never purposefully cause you to feel any unpleasantness whatsoever."

"Thank you both," I said. "Could we please sit back down and converse like civilized people again?"

The three of us sat, but Sydney and Vidocq continued to watch each other with the intensity of a pair of prize fighters entering the boxing ring.

Charles returned to the room and could easily discern that something was amiss. His concerned gaze landed on me; and I shook my head slightly, hopefully conveying that the situation wasn't serious.

He remained standing as he made his announcement. "Mr. Lorry has just informed me that Dr. Manette's body has been stolen."

CHAPTER 10

I was surprised Charles made this announcement in front of Sydney rather than waiting until he, Vidocq, and I were alone. But since Mr. Lorry had brought the news, I supposed Charles thought he might as well have told us all since Sydney would find out soon enough anyway.

"What does this mean?" I asked. "Who would take my father's body?"

"Unfortunately, the robbing of graves has become a common way of making extra money," Sydney said.

The three men stared at one another, none wanting to be the one to further elaborate. I did so for them.

"I'm aware grave robbers often steal cadavers from cemeteries to sell to medical schools. Yet, I find it nearly impossible to accept that my father might have suffered such a fate." I placed a hand over my racing heart. "Mr. Lorry is surely misinformed."

"You've paled considerably from the shock," Vidocq said. "One of us should escort you upstairs, *n'est-ce pas?*"

I nodded. "Yes, please."

"If you gentlemen will excuse us, I'll take my wife up to our room." Charles came over, took my hand, and helped me to my feet.

Truly shocked and upset, I was certain the removal of Dr. Manette's body from its grave was the work of silverfish rather than grave robbers. But why would they do such a thing?

I asked Charles that very question as soon as we were alone in our room.

"I have no idea," he said. "And we can't be a hundred percent sure that the body was stolen by the silverfish. If you'll recall, Jerry Cruncher was a grave robber in the original version of *A Tale of Two Cities.*"

A few minutes later, there was a tap on our bedroom door. Charles opened it to find Vidocq standing in the hallway.

"Everyone is decent, *oui?*" he asked.

"Yes." Charles stood aside and gestured for the other man to enter the room, closing the door behind him.

"So Vidocq is alone in being indecent?" he asked, arching one eyebrow.

"Not indecent," I said. "Incorrigible."

He grinned. "Our Mr. Carton is off to roust the known grave robbers."

"Did he mention Jerry Cruncher?" Charles asked.

"Not in so many words; but as Cruncher is known to

be a grave robber in the initial manuscript, it stands to reason it will be he who is rousted, *non?*"

"Charles and I are trying to determine whether this body theft was the work of the silverfish or simply Mr. Cruncher being true to his character," I said.

"I imagine we'll know that when we speak with Mr. Cruncher," Charles said.

"*Exactement.* I must, however, voice another concern while the three of us are able to speak privately."

"What's that?" I placed my hand on the bedpost, feeling I might need its support to remain standing should I receive another shock so soon on the heels of discovering Dr. Manette's body had been stolen.

"It's this Sydney Carton." Vidocq shook his head. "He loves you with the utmost passion, *ma petite.*"

Releasing the breath I'd been holding, I said, "That isn't anything new. Sydney's love for Lucie is the very crux of the redemptive arc of *A Tale of Two Cities.* If Sydney hadn't loved Lucie, he wouldn't have taken Charles' place at the guillotine."

"Precisely." Vidocq punctuated the word with an upraised index finger. "This Sydney Carton would not do that. This man would help destroy Charles so he could swoop in and be the hero in Lucie's life. That is why I made it abundantly clear to him that the Defarges want Lucie dead as well as Charles."

"Sharp thinking, Vidocq. Thank you." Charles rubbed his forehead. "I, too, am aware that this Sydney doesn't look at Lucie in the reverential way a man with a noble, unrequited love would observe her. Rather, he gazes at her like a man desperate to possess her."

"Familiar with that look, are you, *mon ami?*" Vidocq chuckled.

Ignoring Vidocq's playful gibe, I said, "Sydney did ask me if I was having second thoughts about my marriage at the reception, and he even offered to have our union annulled. But what difference does it make? All we have to do to reset the story is find Dr. Manette's killer, right? Then it won't matter what Sydney Carton does or doesn't do."

Vidocq and Charles shared a glance that I couldn't interpret.

"What aren't you two telling me?" I'd had a private word with Vidocq and received confidential information. Maybe Charles had done so as well.

Raising his thick brows at Charles, Vidocq spread his hands.

"This story is progressing much too fast," Charles said. "You and I discussed this already when I received the letter from Gabelle."

"But there's more to it," I said flatly.

"Correct. The silverfish are desperate to get Charles Darnay to the guillotine," Vidocq said. "We need Sydney Carton on our side to ensure that does not happen."

"Then I'll speak with him."

"And say what?" Charles asked. "This incarnation of Sydney Carton wants to be the man to make you happy whereas the original willingly died so that you could be happy with your husband and remaining child—and the child you might one day name after him for the sacrifice he made."

"Our only recourse is to solve this mystery and have the book reset before the Defarges and the silverfish get Charles into Paris," Vidocq said.

My head was beginning to ache. "I really do need to lie down for a few minutes."

"You should, *ma petite*. You are looking quite pale." Vidocq turned from me to Charles. "And you should stay with her. I'll walk about town for a bit and see what I can learn."

After Vidocq left the room, I sank onto the side of the bed and unbuttoned my shoes. "You don't have to babysit me. I'll be fine."

"I know you will, but I want to stay with you." Charles went around to the other side of the bed. "Vidocq will do some excellent sleuthing, and it won't hurt for us to take a short break."

I took my shoes off and lay down on the bed. Charles stretched out beside me.

"I know we should be discussing the case," I said, rolling onto my side to face him. "But I really don't want to right now."

"Neither do I." He gently brushed back a strand of hair that had fallen into my eyes.

"What do you miss most about life back home? Other than Cooper, of course."

"Besides Cooper, I miss modern plumbing." He

smiled. "I miss grocery stores and electricity and telephones."

Thinking about the cell phone that was practically an extra appendage when I was back in North Carolina, I felt a wave of guilt. Charles would likely be amazed by the new technology that had been developed over the years he'd been in Literatia.

"You have to go back home, Charles. You've been away for far too long and sacrificed too much of your life for Literatia."

"Not for Literatia." He lowered his eyes. "For my son."

"It's time for you to go home." I took his hand. "I'm going to find a way."

He raised my fingers to his lips and kissed them. "Let me hold you, and let's take a nap. I have a feeling we won't have too many peaceful moments ahead of us on this journey."

Nodding, I snuggled against his chest. Despite the calmness and the quiet and the fact that I could hear Charles' heart thumping rhythmically next to me, I felt anything but peaceful. The silverfish were determined to execute Charles Darnay, and in doing so, kill Matthew. I vowed to myself to find a way to keep that from happening and to get Matthew safely out of Literatia. He'd made the sacrifice long enough. It was my turn.

I AWOKE to a frantic pounding on the bedroom door. Charles leapt out of bed and was en route to answer it when Vidocq barged into the room.

"We must—you and I—" He waved his hand back and forth between himself and Charles. "—speak privately on a most urgent matter."

I'd already sat up and was pulling on my shoes. "Oh, no, you don't. You're not leaving me in the dark. What's going on?"

"Oh, *ma chere. C'est horrible!*"

"English please," Charles said.

"The silverfish...Cruncher...they've contrived to make you look guilty."

Charles took Vidocq firmly by the shoulders. "Calm down, man. They're trying to make me look guilty of what—Dr. Manette's murder?"

Vidocq shook his head. "Not you. Gia."

Reader, I jumped off the bed and nearly fell out of the shoe I hadn't finished buttoning.

"What the ever-loving cuss? They're framing *me*? How? I was nowhere near the kitchen when Dr. Manette was murdered."

Vidocq stepped away from Charles and gently propelled me back toward the edge of the bed. My knees gave way, and I sat.

"The constable is coming for you." Vidocq knelt and finished buttoning my shoe.

"On the basis of what evidence?" Charles demanded.

"When Mr. Cruncher liberated Dr. Manette's body

from its confines, he found Lucie's brooch clasped in the doctor's right hand."

"That's ridiculous." Charles paced the room. "How can it be proven that it's Lucie's brooch? And even if it *is* positively identified as hers, there are numerous witnesses who will testify to Lucie's being in the salon at the time of the murder."

Vidocq gulped as his eyes locked onto mine.

Realization dawned as I reached out to pat his shoulder. "Let me guess. The blackbird is a witness against me."

He closed his eyes as he nodded, and the steel jaws of fear clamped down on me.

"What do I do?" I whispered.

Charles came to the side of the bed, lifted me onto my feet, and cradled me against him. "We'll fight. I'll do whatever I have to do to get you out of this. You'll—"

His words were cut off by the sound of the constable and his men thundering up the stairs.

"Lucie Darnay, you are under arrest for the murder of your father, Dr. Alexandre Manette."

Oh, crap, Reader. I was a hundred percent certain I'd never survive modern jail, much less ye olde gaol of the 1700s. But, at least, I wouldn't be staying long if the silverfish had their way —I'd be executed as soon as possible.

CHAPTER 11

Cold. Dismal. Small. Wretched.

That was both how my cell looked and how I felt sitting in it. Both Charles and Vidocq had vehemently protested my arrest, but it hadn't done any good. Charles had shouted assurances that he'd get justice for me as I was led away. Now here I sat on a stone slab wondering what would happen next.

I'd known the silverfish were eager to get rid of Charles, a/k/a Matthew, but I hadn't realized they considered me enough of a threat to bother with. I'd apparently made an impression on them with my work in *Jane Eyre*.

Thinking back to *A Tale of Two Cities*, it occurred to me that Lucie had never been in any real danger in the book. Unlike Charles, she'd never stood trial, been imprisoned, or sentenced to death. Dr. Manette's murder corrected that oversight for the silverfish.

A jailer informed me I had a visitor. Expecting Charles, I was surprised to see Sydney Carton approaching the cell.

"Hello." I stood and walked toward the bars. "It appears good news travels fast."

He reached out to me between the bars, and his hands were shaking nearly as much as mine were. "I'm so terribly sorry."

I felt obliged to take his hands. "Can you help me? You know I'd never harm my father."

"Of course, I know that. You could never hurt anyone."

"It's that Madame Grievous," I said. "She's the one falsely testifying against me. Didn't you tell me she's friends with Monsieur and Madame Defarge?"

"I did. Do you think they're behind this travesty?"

"Absolutely. I believe they were unsure if they could execute me solely on the basis of my marriage to Charles, so they found another way to ensure my death."

"I won't let that happen," he said. "I promise you."

I scoffed. "Forgive me if I'm not comforted by everyone's reassurances."

"Everyone's?"

"Yes. Yours, Charles', Vidocq's." I sighed. "I know all of you mean well, but these…people…are determined to see me dead."

"I swear I'll save you." He squeezed my hands before letting them go and stepped back. "I'll return as soon as I have news." He was walking away as the jailer was coming to get him.

I sat back down on the slab and questioned my motives for being open—to an extent—with Sydney Carton. After all, I knew Charles and Vidocq were doing everything humanly possible to get me out of my dire predicament, and they were familiar with my true enemies.

Maybe *humanly* possible was the key. I supposed I wanted a *character* who'd always been a part of this narrative—changed though he may now be—to lend a helping hand. I wasn't completely confident he'd be able to help, but he might at least buy Charles, Vidocq, and me some time to solve Dr. Manette's murder and reset the book.

MY NEXT VISITOR—AN hour or so after Sydney had left— was Vidocq.

"Where's Charles?" I asked.

I'm sorry, Reader, but I was a little put out that my pretend husband and not-so-pretend crush hadn't rushed to the jail to rain more assurances, love, and devotion down on me. After all, he'd been imprisoned the first time I'd met him in Jane Eyre, *and I'd worked tirelessly to free him. And I'd taken him candy.*

"Charles is right now with Jerry Cruncher—" He lowered his voice. "—who is not a silverfish, by the way, to get him to admit that someone paid him to say he found your brooch in the hand of Dr. Manette."

Okay, Reader, sorry. If jumping to conclusions were an Olympic event, I'd have a gold medal. Maybe two.

"What about Madame Grievous?" I put my fingertips to my temples. "Has anyone seen her?"

"Mr. Stryver, the lawyer, says Sydney Carton is out looking for her. With her being a silverfish and him not, however, I don't know how much good it will do." He motioned me forward so he could lower his voice to a whisper, and I could still hear. "Charles is also petitioning Josephine to get you out of the book. It's the only way to be certain of your safety."

"I refuse to leave," I whispered back. "You know as well as I do how imperative it is that Charles be the one to return home to North Carolina this time. Besides, without me here, Charles might die before the murder can be solved and the book reset."

Vidocq was so incensed by what I'd said that he forgot himself and raised his voice. "Do you believe Vidocq would allow such a thing to happen?"

"Of course not. I'm upset, that's all. I've never been in jail before."

He clucked his tongue. "I forget not everyone is as full of the adventure as Vidocq. Perhaps I can aid in your escape."

"Since I've nowhere to go outside the confines of this book, how about you and Charles solve Dr. Manette's murder and reset the manuscript?"

"You know I am already hard at work on that. I overlook your unbecoming attitude and request that you tell me everything you can recall about the day of the murder."

Starting with my entry into the book at the back of the church on the arm of Dr. Manette, I gave Vidocq a play-by-play of the wedding, the carriage ride, the reception, the murder, and the aftermath—including the next morning when the Defarges called at the house.

"Do you recall having on the brooch allegedly found in Dr. Manette's hand at any time?" he asked.

"No. I haven't worn any jewelry other than this." I held up the back of my left hand to display the simple gold band Charles had placed on my ring finger during our wedding ceremony.

"May I see that?"

I removed the ring and placed it on Vidocq's outstretched palm. He grasped the ring between the thumb and forefinger of his opposite hand, twisted it around, and smiled.

"It is as I suspected—a posy ring."

"A what?" I frowned.

"Have you not previously removed the ring and examined it? Look. There is an inscription inside." He returned the ring, and I squinted at the words engraved inside it.

I think you were sent to me by Heaven.

"Posy rings bear a poetic verse or personal message of significance to the bride and groom," Vidocq said. "You will naturally recognize the words spoken to Mr. Carton by the seamstress as together they faced the guillotine."

I nodded, not trusting myself to speak. The tears that threatened burned my nose and made swallowing difficult. Remorse for thinking Charles wasn't doing everything he could to help me made me unable to meet Vidocq's eyes as I slid the ring back onto my finger.

"No time for sorrow or self-recrimination, *ma petite*. Do you have more to tell me?"

Clearing my throat before speaking, I said, "I don't believe so."

"Have you had any visitors or strange encounters since you've been here in the jail?"

"My only visitor was Sydney. When he reached for my hands, they were trembling almost as much as mine were."

Vidocq's brows shot up. "Sydney Carton reached for your hands, and you took them?"

"Yes. I took his overture to be a gesture of friendship and comfort," I said. "Should I have refused to clasp his outstretched hands?"

"Perhaps. Perhaps not. We shall see."

Vidocq knew from our time together in *Jane Eyre* that my living in modern-day America had led me to grow up without the social constraints of 18th Century women.

"What do you mean, 'we shall see'?" I asked. "I thought it would be all right since the handholding was done under unusual circumstances."

"I mean what I say, *ma petite*. We shall see how Mr.

Carton interprets your actions. He is in love with Lucie Manette Darnay. The fact that you allowed him to hold your hands might suggest to him that you are also in love with him."

I turned down the corners of my mouth. "Are you afraid this could lead Sydney to sacrifice himself for *me* rather than for Charles? I mean, he could confess to the murder in order to allow me to be set free."

"That is what we must wait to see," Vidocq said. "A false confession would only hinder us in solving Dr. Manette's murder. Let us hope Mr. Carton will instead help us find the true culprit."

When Vidocq left, I went back to the cold stone slab, turned my face to the dingy gray wall, and curled into the fetal position. With my right hand, I rotated the gold band on my left and considered the inscription.

I think you were sent to me by Heaven.

I felt certain Charles had managed to have the ring inscribed knowing I would soon be joining him in Literatia and in what capacity. And I couldn't feel less like a godsend at the moment.

Despite my uncomfortable position, I dozed into a fitful, dream-filled sleep.

I imagined I was back in North Carolina in the restaurant where I'd dined with Connie such a short time ago. Although her nails had actually been short and unvarnished at lunch, now they were long and painted blood red. I couldn't help but notice them as she kept making elaborate gestures as she talked.

The waiter brought our food out in antique domed silver servers and placed them in front of us. He removed the lid from Connie's with a flourish, and I saw that it contained a ball of white yarn and a pair of knitting needles. She immediately picked up the needles and began to knit. As she did so, the yarn turned from white to a red as deep as the polish on her fingernails.

"Madame?" The waiter was looking at me.

"What?"

"Would you like me to reveal your dish?" he asked.

A knot of dread gathered in the pit of my stomach. "N-no."

Connie laughed, her knitted red yarn now covering half the table. "Aw, go on, Gia. It'll be fun."

Without any further input from me, the waiter lifted the lid to reveal Charles' severed head.

I jerked awake, my body drenched in a cold sweat. I couldn't simply give up and allow myself to be a victim. That would surely lend itself not only to my destruction, but to the detriment of Charles and *A Tale of Two Cities*. I had to do *something*. But what?

CHAPTER 12

After walking in circles around the cell both clockwise and counterclockwise, I came to the conclusion that my best bet would be to have a discussion with either Josephine or Cooper. I imagined it would have to be Josephine, unless she'd been mistaken about the severity of Cooper's condition.

The only time I'd ever communicated with Cooper while I was in Literatia was shortly after I'd arrived in the world of *Jane Eyre*. I'd been sitting alone in a carriage when I'd found a note from Cooper in my reticule. Upon reading the note, I'd answered aloud as if he could hear me. Surprisingly enough, he had.

We'd had an entire conversation with me speaking and his answers appearing on the paper like some sort of magic texting device. When we'd finished communicating, the note had turned to ash here in Literatia—Cooper had burned it in North Carolina.

I needed to figure out how to initiate a conversation. Maybe anything written in Literatia would show up as part of the book I was in.

"Jailer!" I called. "Would you come here please?"

He didn't answer, but I heard his heavy boots thudding on the floor as he stomped down the hallway toward my cell. When he reached me, he still said nothing but merely looked at me with contempt. As far as I could tell, this man wasn't a silverfish. Under the circumstances, I couldn't be sure whether that was a good thing or a bad thing. Probably good because I preferred to avoid those nasty silverfish at all costs.

"I'd like some paper and a writing instrument please."

Sneering, he said, "Begging your pardon, my lady, but we are all out of your personal stationery."

Taking his sarcasm in stride, I said, "Whatever you have will be fine. I'm not asking for anything fancy."

He guffawed as he turned to leave.

"Wait! Won't you please allow me to write a note?"

"No." He kept walking.

"Will you contact someone for me then?"

This time, he didn't even answer my question.

I stomped my foot and regretted it instantly. The pain that shot up my leg reminded me of how unyielding the floor was. Limping back across the cell, I sagged onto the stone slab.

Now what? I supposed I could cry and feel sorry for myself. But that wouldn't help matters. If I could find something with a sharp edge to it, maybe I could scratch a message onto the wall.

Knowing the cloth-covered buttons down the front of my bodice were metal, I set about trying to pull off the lowest button.

I was having no luck when I heard a deep, rich voice say, "Lucie."

Jerking my head up, I saw Charles standing outside my cell.

Reader, instead of showing him the immeasurable gratitude I was feeling, I'm ashamed to say I acted like a jerk.

"It's about time!" I wailed as I sprinted to the bars. "I thought you'd deserted me!" My *waaah* would have made Lucy Ricardo proud. I supposed if we were sharing a moniker we might as well share histrionics.

"Hush, darling," Charles said. "You must know I'd never turn my back on you. I've been doing my dead-level best to get you out of this place."

I sniffled. "I know."

He handed me a monogrammed handkerchief through the bars, and I wiped my eyes.

"I'm sorry," I said. "I am grateful. It's just that I'm also scared."

"I know you are."

"You are too. I see it in your eyes."

He didn't deny it. "I wish I could take your place."

"What evidence do they have against me?"

Reaching through the bars, he took my hand. "I leaned heavily on Jerry Cruncher, but all he could tell me was that a man he'd never seen before paid him to say a brooch—provided to him by that same stranger—was clutched in the hand of Dr. Manette when Cruncher opened the grave."

"That doesn't make a bit of sense. The constable would have checked to make sure there was nothing in the victim's hands at the scene of an attack. Right?"

"One would believe so, yes," Charles said. "But you must never forget that nearly everything in this manuscript has been corrupted by the silverfish."

"You and I made short work of Bertha Rochester's murder investigation in *Jane Eyre,* and the silverfish are determined to see us fail this time no matter what." My eyes filled with more tears of self-pity, but I resolutely blinked them away. "Tell me about the other evidence. Since Cruncher is willing to testify that a man gave him the brooch and paid him to lie about where he'd discovered it, the prosecution's case must rest on the Blackbird —I mean, Madame Grievous."

"It does. We have witnesses willing to testify that they saw you speaking with Madame Grievous at the time Miss Pross screamed and alerted us all to the fact that she'd found Dr. Manette bleeding on the kitchen floor." His hand tightened around mine. "I'll get you out of that cell, darling, one way or another."

I know what he was intimating—if the trial went badly, he meant to contact Cooper or Josephine and have me taken out of the book. I couldn't let that happen. I'd vowed to get Charles back to North

Carolina, and I had every intention of keeping that promise.

"Everything will work out," I said. "It has to. When is my trial?"

"Tomorrow."

My stomach recoiled at this news, and I had to fight a wave of nausea. "That soon?"

"I'm afraid so. The silverfish are working quickly—but so are we."

THE NEXT TIME I heard footsteps approaching my cell, I put on a brave face and even managed to smile slightly as I went to greet my visitor. That smile fell when I saw that it was Madame Grievous who'd come to see me.

Reader, my legs practically turned to jelly, but I'd have died before I let this evil creature know I was scared.

"What are you doing here?" I raised my chin slightly.

"I heard you were in a spot of trouble and thought maybe I could help you."

"You could indeed." I inclined my head. "You could tell the truth—that I was speaking with you when Miss Pross screamed."

Her thin lips curled into a closed-mouthed smile. "I could indeed inform the judge that the two of us were having a *tete-a-tete* when Miss Pross sounded the alarm. But, my dear, we have no idea how long Dr. Manette lay on that floor before he was discovered. Who knows where you were when the murder took place?"

"You and your lies will not prevail against me."

I was bluffing, Reader. She and her lies might very well be the death of me.

"That remains to be seen," she said. "I'm here to offer you a deal. Convince Charles to go to Paris with the intention of freeing Gabelle, and we will let you go."

Shaking my head, I said, "I don't trust you."

"You don't have much of a choice. Have Charles go to Paris after the trial, and you will be exonerated." She flipped her wrists. "*And* you may have your pen and paper which I expect you wanted to use to ask your curator to get you out of this book."

"How'd you know about the pen and paper?" I frowned. "I didn't think that jailer was a silverfish."

"He isn't, but a few coins can buy me all the information I want." She stepped closer to the bars. "Take my advice. Do as I ask, then have yourself removed from *A Tale of Two Cities,* and never meddle in the affairs of Literatia again. Otherwise, you will die." She gave me a broad smile now, allowing me to see the silverfish crawling through her teeth.

I somehow managed to suppress a shudder, and I remained silent. She thought I wanted to contact Cooper to have him pull me out of the book when, in fact, I wanted to ask what I needed to do to get Charles out. I felt it was better to let Madame Grievous have the wrong idea.

She blew out a foul-smelling breath and said, "I'll give you tonight to contemplate your options. Before the trial, I'll send someone to get your decision."

As soon as she walked off, my legs gave way, and I crumped to the floor.

So this was their plan—frighten me into sacrificing Charles and then leave Literatia forever. While I couldn't honestly say I wasn't scared half out of my mind, if they wanted a fight, I'd give it to them.

CHAPTER 13

Dear, sweet Reader, I taxed my poor brain for hours trying to figure out how I was going to wage war on an amalgamated group of book-eating silverfish. I got bupkis.

I was sitting on my slab half strategizing and half feeling pitiful when Charles and Vidocq arrived.

"Hallelujah!" I hurried over to the bars of my cell. "The cavalry!"

Both men laughed. They obviously didn't realize I was serious.

Charles took a small packet tied with string from his coat pocket. "Are you hungry?"

"Yes, but food can wait." I took the packet and placed it on my slab. "I truly appreciate the food, but there are things you must know. Can one of you bribe the jailer to leave us alone? Trust me—I know he can be bought. That's why we need to get rid of him and make sure he isn't eavesdropping."

"I'll take care of it," Vidocq said.

He left, and Charles pierced me with a questioning look.

"I won't say a word until I know the jailer won't be repeating what I say to Madame Grievous." I sat on the floor. "Thank you again for the food."

Charles joined me on the floor. "You're welcome. I know prisoners aren't fed well."

I reached through the bars, and he took my hand.

Vidocq returned and assured me that the jailer had left for fifteen minutes. "I don't trust him to give us more than ten," he said, as he looked dubiously at the dusty floor before taking a seat. "Speak quickly."

"Madame Grievous came to see me. She offered to speak in my defense at the trial provided I convince Charles to go to Paris, have Cooper remove me from this book, and never meddle in the affairs of Literatia again. She knew I'd asked the jailer for a pen and paper—she told me she'd bribed him for information."

"Why did you ask for pen and paper, *ma petite?*" Vidocq's eyes held a challenge.

I struggled with what to say. If only Vidocq were present, I'd have no trouble telling him the absolute truth. But Charles was here. I didn't want him to know how desperately I wanted to get him out of Literatia. He'd only try to convince me to save myself and to not worry about him.

On the other hand, I might be convicted of murder

tomorrow and sentenced to death. This might be my only chance.

Taking a deep breath, I dived in. "I asked for the pen and paper to attempt to contact Cooper or Josephine. Madam Grievous correctly guessed that, but she doesn't know why. She believes I was going to ask them to pull me out of the book."

"And your real reason?" Charles asked.

"I need to know how to save you." I squeezed his hand. "Please, Matthew—" I resorted to using his real name. "—tell me how to get you home."

"It's not—" He sighed. "Our time is short. The most important thing right now is to save you."

I looked from Charles to Vidocq.

"He's right," Vidocq said. "We will address the other concern after you are freed from this cell."

"I've thought about this trial and these charges against me ever since Madame Grievous left," I said. "The woman has me over a barrel. If I don't do what she wants —and I absolutely will not—then she'll testify against me, and I'll be sentenced to death."

"Ah, but if you lie and agree to her terms, you will be acquitted, *n'est-ce pas?*" Vidocq spread his hands. "She attempts to play you, and yet, you beat her at her own game."

"If I thought it would be that simple, that's exactly what I'd do; but she's bound to have taken precautions to ensure I don't double cross her. I imagine she trusts me even less than I trust her."

"Lucie's right," Charles said. "If she takes Madame Grievous' deal, the silverfish will see to it that Lucie keeps her part of the bargain. But I'm at a loss to ascertain what alternative we have." His eyes bore into mine. "You must take the deal."

"I will not!"

"It's the only way we can be sure you'll live to—"

"No!" I interrupted. "The first time I met you, you were on death row. You had five days to live. And yet here you sit."

"This is different," he said.

"It isn't." I gently pulled my hand away and stood. "You trusted me with your life. I'm trusting you with mine. Solve the mystery of Dr. Manette's murder and reset the book."

Charles and Vidocq got to their feet.

"I hear the jailer," Vidocq said quietly. "He is back. No more privileged conversation."

"Gia, please take the deal," Charles whispered.

I merely shook my head.

The jailer returned. I couldn't see him because he stopped at the end of the hallway.

"Time's up, laddies. Bid your lady goodnight." His footsteps retreated.

Charles reached through the bars. When I took his hands, he tugged me closer and managed to kiss me on the lips.

"May I get one of those?" Vidocq asked.

I grinned. "I don't believe you're his type, *mon cher.*"

"Oh, get over here, you, and let me hold your hand for a second at least."

I stepped over to Vidocq and gave him my hand. He sandwiched it between both of his, and I felt something stony against my palm. He winked.

"Thank you," I said. "Both of you. It means so much to me that you're here and that you're fighting for me."

Vidocq released my hand, and I shoved it into the pocket of my skirt to deposit the object he'd given me.

"One last time," Charles whispered. "Take the deal Madame Grievous is offering."

"One last time," I whispered back. "Solve the case."

As soon as they were gone, I walked over to the slab where I'd placed the packet of food. With my back to the bars of the cell, I withdrew the object Vidocq had given me. It was a shard of charcoal. I couldn't suppress a smile.

"Good old Vidocq."

I untied the string and opened the paper packet of food to find corn pone, an apple, and some figs. I ate the corn pone as I was deciding what to say to Josephine. Then I smoothed the paper out onto the slab and picked up the shard of charcoal.

As the thought *here goes nothing* went through my head, I wrote, "Josephine, this is Gia. I desperately need to communicate with you."

I waited for what felt like two hours but couldn't have been more than a couple of minutes.

The words *I'm here* appeared on the paper below my greeting.

"How is Cooper?" I wasn't used to writing with charcoal and doing so took longer than I liked.

Being evaluated.

That was cryptic. Still, rather than ask for clarification that she probably wouldn't give, I asked, "How do I get Matthew home? I feel certain you'll agree that he needs to be there with his son."

I do agree, but the silverfish decreed long ago that a member of the Wellington family must be in Literatia at all times.

"But, Josephine, they're trying to kill Matthew and force me out of Literatia forever. If I refuse, they'll kill me too."

It took Josephine longer to respond this time.

Are you being overly dramatic?

"No." In as few words as possible—I was running out of space on my paper—I conveyed what Madame Grievous had told me.

This time it took Josephine so long to reply that I was beginning to think she wasn't going to answer me at all. At last, she said, *How close are you to solving the mystery and resetting the manuscript?*

"We're working on it. Thanks for sending Vidocq."

You're welcome. There was a pause. *I'm afraid that resetting the book is your only hope of everyone getting out of* A Tale of Two Cities *unscathed."*

"And Matthew? How do I get him back home?"

You can't. You aren't a Wellingham.

As I was reading the message, it disappeared along with the rest of Josephine's words. I understood that our conversation was over.

Munching on the apple, I contemplated what she'd said. Cooper was being evaluated? What did that even mean? I felt the fact that she was being cagey about his condition meant he wasn't doing well.

But it was the last thing she'd said that played over and over in my mind.

You aren't a Wellingham.

Could I marry Matthew and then stay in Literatia in his place? For all intents and purposes, the two of us had gotten married in this book. Did that mean anything outside of *A Tale of Two Cities*? Or did we have to be married in our own world for me to become a Wellingham and take Matthew's place? Either way, I doubted he'd be willing to let me stay in his stead. Unless, of course, I told him about Cooper. And I didn't want to do that until the mystery was solved. It would only upset him, especially if he couldn't get back home and check on Cooper himself.

THE NEXT MORNING, I ate my figs. The jailer—a different man from the one who'd been here yesterday—had brought some gritty mush for breakfast. The very sight of it had turned my stomach. Still, that was nothing compared to the way my stomach lurched when I heard footsteps in the hallway.

Only one person—not two. Not likely to be Vidocq or Charles at this time of the morning. I instinctively knew it was either Madame Grievous herself or her lackey who was heading my way.

A tall, attractive man in his mid- to late-twenties stopped outside my cell with an inscrutable smirk on his face. "Well, well, well, as I live and breathe."

Frowning, I asked, "Who are you?"

"Sebastian Connor." He laughed. "You'll soon see the cleverness in my name, but I'm not certain you'll appreciate it."

"Have we met?"

"Sure, we have. Only not in Literatia. You might *look* like Lucie Manette, but I know who you really are." He looked me up and down. "No wonder you were boning up on the French Revolution when we last spoke. Too bad it didn't do you much good."

The dominoes began to tumble.

Sebastian Connor. Sebastian was the name of Connie's cat.

Clink.

Boning up on the French Revolution. "That sounds horrible," Connie had said.

Clink.

Not in Literatia. Either this was Connie, or the person I'd had lunch with a few days ago had been a silverfish impersonating my old college roommate.

Clink.

Sebastian Connor watched in amusement as confusion and then realization washed over my face. He laughed again. "Ah, you're getting there."

"Connie?"

"Ding, ding, ding. We have a winner."

"Is it really you, or are you a silverfish who pretended to be Connie at lunch the other day?"

"Of course, I'm not a silverfish. You don't see any of those slimy things slithering around in my teeth, do you?" He bared all his teeth so I could plainly see that they were blindingly white and free of silverfish.

"But how are you here?"

"The same way you are, sweetie. My client placed me in this book." He rolled his eyes. "Thank goodness it's only temporary."

"But you're a woman."

"Ugh. But, but, but, but." He scoffed. "You're a real newbie to Literatia, aren't you? You don't have to be the same sex as your character, Gia. You could have come into this book as Sydney Carton or Jarvis Lorry had that been what your employer wanted."

The final domino fell. Women were not permitted to practice law in the 1700s.

Clink.

I gave Sebastian/Connie a smirk of my own. "Doesn't it gall you that you couldn't be here as a woman and show all these 18th Century men how brilliant you are?"

"Not in the least. I don't need the validation of a

bunch of fictional characters. All I want is the generous fee my client is paying me."

Well, Reader, her words wiped the goofy little smile off my face. My false bravado, or whatever had caused me to try to bait this person, had come back to bite me. But I now knew that people could be put into books as anyone, and that information could prove to be useful one of these days.

"You know why I'm here," Sebastian said. "Have you come to a decision?"

"I have." I squared my shoulders and stiffened my spine. Back to that false bravado. "I'll attend my trial and hope the truth will win out."

All vestiges of levity left Sebastian's face. "You can't be serious, Gia."

"I am."

"Okay, first off, I'm an ace attorney, and I have the evidence to destroy you. Second, this trial is a straight-up farce. Even if I was a lousy attorney, I'd win."

"I'll take my chances."

"This isn't funny anymore. Do you understand that if you're killed in this book, you'll remain dead?" he asked. "The fictional characters are revived and put back into place when and if the book resets. Humans who die in the book are dead. Period."

"I'm aware of that." Miraculously, my voice didn't quaver.

Sebastian ran a hand down his face. "Do I have to spell this out for you again? You are getting ready to stand trial. You're going to lose the trial, be convicted of murder, and be hanged. Hanged. With a real rope. From real gallows. Where your neck will really be broken. And you will really die. That's not a scenario that *could* or *might* happen—it's what *will* happen. It's going to happen. To you. Take the out."

"I can't."

"You *can*, Gia. You must!" He groaned. "I wish I could reach through those bars and shake you to make you understand. We're friends. I don't want to have you killed."

"But you will." We both knew it was true.

"It's my job."

"Even though you know I've done nothing wrong, you'll do everything in your power to convict me," I said.

"It's my job."

I slowly nodded. "Would you do the same thing in our world? Convict and condemn an innocent person?"

"It's. My. Job."

"Right. Just curious, how much did it cost the silverfish to buy your soul?"

"I warned you. There's nothing more I can do." Sebastian held up his hands, shook his head, and walked away.

I heard him stop about halfway down the hall. I knew he was expecting me to call him back and say I'd reconsidered. I didn't.

CHAPTER 14

I sat on my slab with my knees drawn up to my chin and thought about my years as Connie's roommate. We got along fine then, mainly because I wasn't confrontational. Connie thought she knew best no matter the situation.

Oh, no, Gia! That dress will never do for the spring formal. Here. Borrow this one of mine.

You're thinking of taking tennis for your P. E. elective? That's dumb. Take boxing or karate with me. You might need to defend yourself someday.

That was ironic. The one I currently needed to defend myself from was her. And I couldn't use the knowledge I'd gained from one semester of karate to do it.

Connie had always needed to be right. Granted, she often was. I had chalked the behavior up to Connie's insecurity. Sure, she seemed to have almost too much confidence on the outside; but deep down, she was trying to win everyone's approval—even mine.

Since we'd been paired as roommates by the college, Connie and I had become friends more from necessity than by actually having anything in common. Yet when I had to leave well into my senior year and finish my classes online because Mom had become sick, Connie had sent flowers to our house once a month. She'd also sent a lovely arrangement when Mom had died.

Connie and I had texted and messaged each other on social media occasionally since that time trying to find a convenient opportunity to get together and catch up. We'd finally found that opportunity on the day I was put into *A Tale of Two Cities*. Based on what I knew now, I realized that hadn't been a coincidence.

For the first time, Connie had been more accommodating to me.

"I'll come to you," she'd said. "We'll meet wherever is most amenable to you. Of course, I don't mind the drive —it'll be fun."

That was a side of Connie I'd never seen before. I thought maybe she'd grown up some and overcome her insecurities. Then when we'd met at the restaurant, Connie had been so dismissive of my work that I decided I must've been mistaken—she hadn't changed at all.

But she had to have known already where I worked and how I made my living. In hindsight, I determined it was likely Connie knew not only what book I'd be traveling to later that day but exactly what the silverfish had in store for me when I arrived.

I hadn't given it much thought before now, but I'd been unaware that other people—those not connected with or working for the Gutenberg family—could move in and out of books. The Gutenbergs had been given responsibility over books by the Knights Templar hundreds of years ago, and Matthew and Cooper were in the bloodline. But, given what I'd been told, I'd never considered that the reach of the Silverfish Council could possibly extend beyond Literatia.

It was while I was dwelling on this new information that Sidney Carton came to visit me. I was disappointed to look up and see Sydney. I'd been hoping for Charles, or if not Charles, at least Vidocq. My face must have given me away.

"I imagine you were hoping for someone else," Sydney said.

"Have you come with the identity of the person who actually murdered my father and the evidence to prove it?" I asked. "If not, then yes, I'm hoping for someone who has that information. Otherwise, I'm afraid I must soon face the gallows—a fate I'm woefully unprepared for."

"I swear to you, Lucie, I will not allow you to die. I'm aiding Mr. Stryver with the case."

"Why isn't he here helping me prepare for the trial?"

"I'm here, and there's nothing you must do except tell the truth."

"Oh, really?" I huffed. "The lawyer for the prosecution has already been here taunting me with the fact that Madame Grievous is going to provide damning testimony against me."

Sydney stepped closer and grasped the bars as if it were *he* who was caged instead of me. "What did he say?"

"Precisely what I told you. Now tell me how you and Mr. Stryver intend to defend me."

"We have witnesses who will testify they saw you in the salon at the time your father was murdered."

"And the prosecution has witnesses who will say I was not," I said. "It all comes down to which of you makes the most believable case."

"We will get you out of this ridiculous predicament. Trust me."

"The lawyer for the prosecution is excellent, Sydney. He might very well crush Mr. Stryver."

"What makes you think so?"

"His reputation precedes him." I knew that the silverfish wouldn't have gone outside Literatia for an attorney who wasn't the *crème de la crème*, not when they might've gotten Daniel Webster, Abraham Lincoln, or any number of celebrated lawyers to plead their case.

Unless, of course, those lawyers wouldn't stoop to unscrupulous tactics. Still, there had to be brilliant, dishonest attorneys who'd been written about extensively, so I knew the silverfish had chosen Connie because she was willing and able to get the job done—

and even more likely because she and I had a personal connection.

Had Connie known she'd be prosecuting me when she'd accepted the job? I supposed it didn't matter. She hadn't quit upon learning she'd be arguing to send me to my death, and she'd told me herself less than an hour ago that she would indeed send me to the gallows. To be fair, she *had* told me she didn't want to have to do it and had encouraged me to take Madame Grievous' deal. Still....

"Lucie!"

I jerked my head up and saw Sydney staring at me. He'd apparently called my name more than once. "What?"

"Everything will be all right."

"That's easy for you to say. You're on the other side of those bars."

Reader, I felt a little bad for berating Sydney given the fact that in the original novel, he'd sacrificed himself in Charles Darnay's place. But this was a different Sydney, and I didn't have any confidence in him and Stryver going up against the stacked deck of the silverfish. I was sweating the fact that if Charles, Vidocq, and I couldn't solve the mystery of Dr. Manette's death, I really could die here in Literatia.

"It isn't easy," he said gruffly. "Nothing about this situation is easy. It tears at my heart to see you in that cell."

I merely nodded, not trusting myself to speak.

"One way or another, I will set you free."

Hearing footsteps in the hallway, I involuntarily

shrank back, believing the jailer was coming to take me to the hearing.

But it wasn't the jailer. It was Charles. I slumped against the wall in relief.

"Carton, if you're finished here, may I have a private word with my wife please?" he asked.

Glaring at him from beneath hooded lids, Sydney nodded. "Lucie—"

Charles cleared his throat.

"*Mrs. Darnay*," Sydney amended through clenched teeth, "Mr. Stryver and I will make certain you are acquitted of this crime."

"Thank you." I still had practically no confidence in my legal team whatsoever, but I was eager for Sydney to leave Charles and me alone.

Sydney turned, and after throwing one more baleful glance in Charles' direction, left.

Stepping close to the bars, I held out my hands. Charles took them, raised both to his lips and kissed them. I hadn't realized how badly my hands were shaking until then.

"My poor darling," he whispered. "I never wanted you to be in such a position as this."

"The silverfish planned this before I even came into the book," I said quietly.

He frowned. "What makes you say that?"

"The day I was sent into *A Tale of Two Cities*, I had lunch with my old college roommate, Connie. Well, she's here as Sebastian Connor, and she's prosecuting my case."

"Are you sure?"

"Positive. Connie—or, rather, Sebastian—came to see me and asked me to take Madame Grievous' deal," I said. "I wasn't aware that other people, besides those sent by Cooper and his associates, could enter Literatia. Nor did I know that these silverfish can come into our world."

"They can't."

"Then how did they hire Connie?"

"They had to have reached out to her through some sort of print medium—newspaper ad, letter, flyer." He shook his head. "I don't know for sure."

"But they *did* reach her—my former roommate. It's obvious they intended to make this attack personal and that their goal is to get rid of me."

"You're right," he said. "But that's not going to happen. Let's stay positive."

I narrowed my eyes. "You weren't this optimistic when we last spoke. In fact, you told me to take the deal."

"Vidocq and I spent last night and this morning strategizing. Everything will be okay."

"Did you determine who the real killer is?" I asked. "Was it Miss Pross working with the Defarges? Was it that relative the silverfish invented to get the Defarges to come to England? Or how about the doctor who attended to Dr. Manette? It's possible Dr. Manette wasn't even dead before that guy came along."

"Shh. Don't get yourself all worked up. Stay calm and

rest assured that I absolutely refuse to let any harm come to you." He kissed my hands again. "I've only known you for a short time, although it feels much longer. I'm falling in love with you, Gia."

We maneuvered our heads around so we could kiss between the bars. For me, it felt like a desperate kiss goodbye, of trying to hold onto the last moments of something good. I wondered if it was the same for him.

When he pulled away at last, he attempted to smile. He didn't quite pull it off.

Hearing the heavy footfall of the jailer in the hallway, I quickly whispered, "I love you, Matthew."

He had no chance to respond because the jailer was there to take me away.

CHAPTER 15

In these days before streaming services, trials were a big deal. It was a literal courtroom drama in 3D, no special glasses necessary. If I lived through this ordeal, I could maybe start a popcorn vending service at the courthouse and make a fortune.

Reader, if you thought I was being flippant because I was terrified, you should pat yourself on the back for your astute observation.

The gallery murmured so much when I was ushered into the courtroom that the judge had to call the onlookers down. Still, I heard people saying things like, "It's her—the daughter! I heard she killed the old man for his money." And "Naw, 'e didn't 'ave any money. She kilt 'im to be rid of 'im so she could start 'er new life."

Good to know I had the people on my side. Innocent until proven guilty and all that jazz.

I was seated between Mr. Stryver and Sydney Carton,

and I was relieved to have seen Charles and Vidocq sitting on the front row.

I hadn't noticed Sebastian Connor until he planted both hands on the table in front of me. "Last chance," he said. "Take the deal."

"You will speak with us rather than directly with our client, Mr. Connor," Sydney said.

"I'll speak with whomever I wish," Sebastian said. "If you're truly desirous of helping your client, you will advise her to take the deal the prosecution is offering."

I glanced to my right and saw Madame Grievous front row and center behind the prosecutor's table. She gave me a smug smile.

Sebastian slapped the table in front of me, and I nearly jumped out of my skin.

"Your Honor, counsel for the prosecution is frightening the defendant," Mr. Stryver said.

"I'm merely presenting the defendant with the opportunity to avoid a trial," Sebastian said. "What say you, Mrs. Darnay? Will you accept the deal the prosecution is offering you?"

"I will not," I said. "I'm innocent."

Sebastian's eyes bore into mine.

"I can't do it, Connie," I whispered, shaking my head slightly.

He bent his head lower and mouthed, "Please."

Sebastian's actions brought on another uproar from the gallery.

"What's 'e doing?"

"Seems like Mrs. Darnay is getting coached by the prosecution. Is it because she's such a looker, do you think? Or be there some other reason?"

"Order in this court!" the judge shouted. "Order! Mr. Connor, either go back to your table and state your case immediately, or I will dismiss this matter."

Sebastian straightened, and I ever so briefly touched his hand, a gesture I was sure had gone unnoticed by anyone in the courtroom not sitting at the defense table.

With a sigh, he returned to the prosecutor's table and began to state his case:

"This brooch having been identified as belonging to Lucie Manette Darnay was found in the clasped hand of the victim, Dr. Alexandre Manette. Earlier in the day, Dr. Manette had given his only child—" He turned and gestured toward me. "—Lucie—in marriage to Charles Darnay, born Evremonde. The Evremondes had Dr. Manette thrown into prison unjustly, and the poor man was driven mad by the horrible conditions he was forced to endure in the Bastille and by the fact that he'd been separated from his family and believed them to be dead.

This once brilliant doctor found his only solace in cobbling shoes. I understand, Your Honor, that Dr. Manette learned of his future son-in-law's close family ties to the Evremondes of France—the same family who'd had him imprisoned—just prior to the wedding. Furthermore, Dr. Manette was murdered at the Darnay's wedding reception."

Although Sebastian continued to provide evidence

and/or conjecture against me, I could no longer hear him because Sydney had leaned over and was whispering gruffly in my ear.

"How do you know that man?"

I frowned at him, not intending to answer as I was trying to listen to the prosecution's opening statement.

Not willing to drop the issue, Sydney asked again how I knew Sebastian.

The quickest answer was the truth—Sebastian and I went to school together. But I didn't know whether or not Lucie Manette had attended school. More than likely, she'd had a governess. So I answered, "We used to be friends. I don't suppose we are anymore."

A part of me realized Sebastian was merely doing the job he'd been hired to do. That's why I'd touched his hand. It had been my attempt at an olive branch. And I hoped the gesture might make him go a little easier on me. I highly doubted it, but anything was possible.

"You called him 'Connie,'" Sydney said.

"Yes. Could we talk about this later? I'd like to hear what's being said about me unless you're considering moving to dismiss based on a conflict of interest."

Sydney turned back toward the front of the courtroom in stony silence.

Even if he *was* thinking of objecting to Sebastian on the grounds that the two of us had been friends in the past, I didn't believe the objection would be upheld. There had previously been no Sebastian Connor in *A*

Tale of Two Cities, and he hadn't been friends with Lucie Manette.

"The prosecution will prove that Mrs. Darnay had the motive, means, and opportunity to strike down her father before he could change his mind about her marriage and upset the happy life she sought with Charles Darnay." Sebastian sat down without a look in my direction.

Mr. Stryver stood. "Your Honor, the defense will show that Mrs. Darnay loved her father very much, was a dutiful daughter, and put her father's well-being above her own. After failing to cajole Dr. Manette into accompanying her and her husband to the ship that was to whisk them away on their honeymoon, Mrs. Darnay insisted on returning home to check on her father. Mrs. Darnay is, by the accounts of all who know her, a solicitous young woman. Tell me, Your Honor, how many brides would forego their wedding trip out of concern over leaving their elderly fathers alone?"

Naturally, the judge didn't answer. Mr. Stryver's discourse sounded too goody-goody even to me. Hopefully, he was getting ready to point out how flimsy the prosecution's case was or point the finger at others more likely to want Dr. Manette dead.

Reader, he did no such thing. He sat back down and gave me a nod of satisfaction as if he'd just delivered the Gettysburg Address—which would have been every bit as effective or more so than the drivel he'd spewed over the courtroom.

I peered over my shoulder at Charles and Vidocq

with my eyebrows raised as high as they would go. The expression was meant to convey, "I'm toast!"

Charles gave me a nod of reassurance, and Vidocq smiled. I was glad I was able to keep from rolling my eyes so hard they'd fall out of my head as I faced forward again.

Sydney got to his feet.

Thank goodness! He must be going to give the rest of the opening statement, pointing out that others had far greater motives for wanting Dr. Manette dead. He'll say the evidence against me is laughable.

Striding to the prosecutor's table, Sydney stood ramrod straight in front of Sebastian Connor. "You behaved dishonorably toward my client prior to the beginning of this trial, sir, and I challenge you to a duel."

Reader, my mouth opened so wide, you could have put a baseball in it. Sebastian's did too. Was Sydney out of his mind?

"I in no way acted disrespectfully to your client, you buffoon," Sebastian said. "You're using theatrics in an attempt to disrupt this hearing."

Was he?

Stryver, Charles, Vidocq, and I all stared at each other incredulously as the gallery went berserk. The spectators wanted a show; and if they weren't going to get to see me convicted of murder today, they'd settle for a little bloodshed between the defense and the prosecution.

"Order in this court!" the judge shouted once again. "Order, I say!"

When the gallery had reached an acceptable volume

of clamor, the judge spoke again. "Mr. Connor, choose your weapon."

"What?" Sebastian stood. "Are you seriously going to indulge this fool in his folly, Your Honor?"

"You've been challenged, Mr. Connor. To refuse Mr. Carton outright is to dishonor yourself. How do you wish to proceed?"

Sebastian glared at me as if I'd put Sydney up to challenging him to a duel. I shook my head to indicate I had nothing to do with this madness.

"Mr. Connor?" the judge prompted.

"Pistols." Sebastian swallowed.

"Court is adjourned until tomorrow after the duel between Mr. Carton and Mr. Connor has been completed. Gentlemen, work out the details and advise me of the arrangements before the end of day." The judge nodded at the jailer. "Take the accused back to her cell."

The jailer came to our table, stepped behind Mr. Stryver who still appeared to be as confused as I was, and grasped me by the upper arm. I stood to avoid being jerked to my feet. Not sure if the onlookers were jeering or cheering, and unsure of whether or not it mattered, I kept my eyes on the floor as the jailer led me back to my cell. I didn't even venture a peek at Charles or Vidocq. I knew they'd come to visit me as soon as possible.

U<small>NFORTUNATELY</small>, the first visitor I had upon being returned to my cell was Madame Grievous. I had no idea how she'd gotten there so quickly, but man, she was angry.

"What have you done?" She practically growled the words at me.

Staying safely on my slab and feeling thankful for the bars for once. I said, "I don't know what you're talking about."

"Did you order that besotted oaf to challenge our lawyer to a duel?"

"Of course, not. His actions surprised me as much as they did everyone else."

"I'll bet they did. This is your doing. You've bewitched Carton into attempting to kill the lawyer who was going to send you to the gallows. But make no mistake, dearie, we can find another champion."

She was shaking so badly with rage that several of the silverfish from which she was comprised fell onto the floor. One scurried into my cell and over to where I was sitting. I stomped the nasty creature.

"You will pay for your disrespect." Madame Grievous stormed off.

I was glad. She couldn't get away quickly enough to suit me. I still had the paper and shard of charcoal in my pocket and was considering contacting Josephine to see if she could get Connie out of the book before the duel could take place.

While I was debating that course of action, Connie herself—Sebastian—came to see me.

"Madame Grievous is furious."

"I know." I stood and walked closer to her. "She was just here. She holds me responsible for Sydney challenging you to a duel."

"You aren't?"

"No! I don't wish you any harm. If I contact Josephine, she might be able to take you out of the book before things get worse."

"So that's your plan. Have me taken out of commission." He barked out a mirthless laugh. "The silverfish would never let me get away with such a blatant act of cowardice. I'll see Mr. Carton on the courthouse lawn tomorrow at six a.m."

"Connie, you can't."

"As you're well aware, I'm as stubborn as you are. And I've shot a gun before. Tomorrow, you're likely to be down one attorney."

"Or one friend," I said.

"Dying in Literatia is a risk you're willing to take. So am I."

Charles and Vidocq joined us then.

Sebastian gave them a polite nod. "Gentlemen. I'll leave you to your visit."

I moved even closer to the bars but waited until Sebastian had left to speak. "Sebastian and Madame Grievous think I put Sydney up to challenging Sebastian to a duel."

"Did you?" Vidocq asked. "If so, it was very clever. I wish I'd thought of it myself."

"Of course, I didn't. I don't want Sebastian or Sydney either one to get hurt."

"What made Carton snap?" Charles asked. "I couldn't hear what Sebastian said to you."

"It was nothing, especially nothing that was offensive," I said. "He merely encouraged me to take the deal."

"We heard that part," Vidocq said. "What did he whisper?"

"He stood there staring at me, and I whispered, 'I can't do it, Connie.' He bent his head closer to me and said 'please.' And then I gave his hand a little pat before he walked away." I groaned. "It *was* my fault. Sydney must have seen me touch Sebastian's hand. It was *my* breach of etiquette, not Sebastian's. I was simply trying to reassure Connie that I understood she was just doing her job."

Vidocq rubbed his chin. "You called Sebastian *Connie* and touched his hand, *n'est-ce pas?*"

"Yes."

"And now the duel makes complete sense." His smile encompassed both me and Charles. "Don't you see? Sydney Carton believes he will eliminate another rival for Lucie's affections…or die trying."

CHAPTER 16

I'd asked Vidocq to ask Sydney Carton to come visit me, and Sydney came to my cell about half an hour later.

"Monsieur Vidocq said you wished to see me."

"Yes." I got off the slab and hurried over to the bars. "What were you thinking challenging Sebastian Connor to a duel?"

"I was thinking the man insulted your honor. I will avenge you tomorrow morning."

"I wasn't insulted," I said. "I'm hurt that someone I considered a friend is willing to do his best to send me to the gallows, but I understand he's merely doing the job he was hired to do."

"A true friend would recuse himself as soon as he realized the woman on trial was someone dear to him."

I snorted. "Connie likes me, I suppose, but no one is really dear to Connie except Connie."

Before you think I'd lost my mind, Reader, saying "Connie" over and over was on purpose. I was testing Vidocq's theory.

A muscle worked in Sydney's jaw. "Why do you refer to that man as 'Connie?' It's the name you called him when he was standing at our table."

"It's a nickname. I knew him well, or thought I did, when we were younger." I lowered my eyes. "He believes you challenged him to this duel at my request."

"Not at your request but for you, yes."

"But why? Was it a tactic designed to slow down the trial, as Monsieur Vidocq believes? Are you trying to delay my being sentenced to death?"

"Perhaps that is a secondary motive. The first is as I told you and everyone present in the courtroom—to defend your honor."

Raising my eyes back to his, I said, "I'm not sure Charles would have taken such a bold step."

"I fear he does not love you as I do." He put a hand through the bars.

I took his rough, callused hand. "You have nothing to prove to anyone. Please call off this duel."

He stiffened. "You are afraid I'll harm this man you care for?"

"It's you I'm afraid will get hurt." I closed my eyes tightly as if the thought brought me physical pain. "You could be killed."

"I adore you," he said quietly.

"Then please call off the duel. If something happens

to you, who will defend me? Mr. Stryver? He's sure to see me sentenced to death."

"This isn't my first duel, love. I will be victorious."

"But what if you aren't? I asked.

"Trust me," he said.

"And what about Sebastian Connor? Can I trust you not to kill him?"

"I'll do no more than draw first blood." He ran his thumb over my hand. "Will you kiss me for luck?"

Vidocq strolled into the hallway. "*Bon chance* tomorrow, Mr. Carton. Good luck." He looked from Sydney to me. "Am I interrupting the private moment?"

"No," I said quickly.

Sydney had already drawn back his hand, and he stepped away from the bars. "Thank you for your well wishes, Monsieur Vidocq. Rest assured nothing untoward was transpiring between the lady and me." Turning his somber gaze back to me, he said, "Goodbye."

"Goodbye and good luck."

Vidocq waited a couple of minutes giving Sydney time to leave the jail before he spoke. "Thanks to the opportunistic nature of the jailer, I heard everything. As I expected, Mr. Carton was bold in expressing his love for you."

"I hadn't expected that," I said. "I thought men from this era were only brazen like that in historical romance novels, not Dickens' classics."

"Pish posh. Our Mr. Carton does not realize he is a character in a novel. He is merely a man in love. And if men in love were not, as you say, *brazen like that*, we would have no modern era." He laughed. "I have made you blush."

"You'd better knock it off before Sydney challenges *you* to a duel."

"He would regret that, *ma petite*. Vidocq is a dueler *par excellence*."

Shaking my head, I said, "Totally incorrigible. On a more serious note, I'm glad Charles wasn't lying in wait with you and hearing the things Sydney and I said to each other."

"He would know full well you were playing the part as we planned, the part designed to determine whether or not Sydney is the murderer of Dr. Alexandre Manette."

"I know this is a different Sydney Carton from the original character, but I find it nearly impossible to believe he'd kill Lucie's father. What outcome could he hope to achieve by that?"

"An outcome similar to that sought by the silverfish," Vidocq said. "The desire to pin the murder on another so that he can have what he wants. The silverfish want Literatia to themselves and are willing to do anything to make that happen. Sydney Carton wants you to himself and will attempt to have you by any means necessary."

"As you pointed out, the silverfish are making a tremendous effort to remove the Wellinghams and their associates from Literatia. What makes you think they didn't kill Dr. Manette themselves?"

"It's possible, but I find it more likely that they merely saw an opportunity to work a situation to their advantage."

"So what do we do now?" I asked.

"We do as mankind has done from the beginning of time. We wait and see what happens next."

"I hate wait and see."

He chuckled. "As do I, *ma petite*, but what alternative do we have?" He tapped his cheek with his forefinger before pressing the side of his face to the bars.

I gave him a peck on the cheek. "You're living dangerously, you saucy Frenchman."

"Always. Charles will be here soon with some food for you."

"That's good to know. I'm hungry." I paused. "Will it be wrapped in paper again, do you imagine?"

"Most likely." He arched a brow. "You wish to converse with Josephine again?"

"Possibly. I was going to ask her to extract Connie from the book, but Connie refuses to go."

"It wouldn't work anyway," he said. "The silverfish brought her in. They must take her out." He squinted at me. "What other reason have you for conversing with Josephine? Vidocq knows there is something more."

I smiled. "A girl should have *some* secrets, *n'est-ce pas?*"

CHARLES BROUGHT a basket filled with treats for us to share. Apparently, he and Vidocq had as much bribe money as Madame Grievous had, so the jailer hadn't forbidden our picnic. Why they weren't using the bribe funds to spring me from this joint was beyond me. That's the question I posed to Charles as he was spreading a cloth onto the floor outside my cell.

"I wish it was that easy." He smoothed the cloth. "But the jailer is only a small cog in a large wheel. He can be paid to look the other way while we have an extended visit, and any information he gleans is for sale, but he cannot pervert the course of justice without paying the consequences himself."

We both sat on the floor. Charles reached into the basket and handed me something soft and round wrapped in plain paper. I soon discovered the object was a roll, and I was as happy to have it as I was for the paper folded around it.

"Jam or honey?" Charles asked.

The jam appeared to be strawberry, so I asked for that.

Charles handed me the jar and a small spatula.

"Thanks. I tried to talk Sydney into calling off the duel," I said. "I also attempted to convince Connie to let me see if there was any way Josephine could get her out of the book, but she refused. Vidocq said that couldn't happen anyway—that the person who brought you into Literatia must be the one to take you out."

"That's true, for the most part."

I spread jam onto my roll. "What about you? Would Cooper have to be the one to take you out of *A Tale of Two Cities*?"

"Cooper or Josephine." He unwrapped a roll, tore it open, and began spreading honey on it. "It's more about point of origin than a person. I must return to the library at Smithmore Manor, same as you. Connie would have to return to whatever portal the silverfish brought her through."

"I see. How many portals are there?"

"I have no idea."

I bit into my roll. The jam was more tart than what I was accustomed to, but it was really tasty. As I ate, I thought about Cooper and his condition. My employer could die without seeing his father in over forty years. I couldn't let that happen.

Charles poured each of us a glass of wine and handed mine through the bars.

Before speaking, I took a sip of the wine for courage. "You need to go home."

"Not yet," he said. "I've paid the jailer to allow me to visit you for an hour."

"I'm not talking about the home in this book. I mean Smithmore. You need to go."

Something in my voice must have alarmed Charles because he grew still. "What aren't you telling me?"

"You know that when I came here, Josephine sent me. That's because Cooper wasn't feeling well."

"So you said. You gave no indication it was anything serious, though. What's wrong with him?"

"I'm not sure." That was true. At this point, I didn't think anyone was aware of the gravity or lack thereof of Cooper's condition. "The evening Vidocq arrived, we both felt as though there was something he wasn't telling us." I took another swig of the sour wine. "A note fell from his pocket, and when I picked it up, I read that Josephine was afraid Cooper might have had a stroke."

Charles looked as if I'd slapped him. "And you didn't tell me immediately?"

"Vidocq and I didn't want you to be overcome with worry before we could solve Dr. Manette's murder and get you out of this book and back home."

He began packing up the basket. "I have to go."

"I'm sorry. I should've told you as soon as I knew."

"Yes," he said. "You should have." He handed me another roll and an apple. "Here. Enjoy them. I'll see you tomorrow."

"Charles, please."

But his long strides had already taken him halfway up the hall by then, and he didn't stop. I didn't blame him.

Gathering my food, I stood and went over to the stone slab. Turning my back to the cell bars, I got out my charcoal, sat down, and wrote to Josephine.

"I'm sorry, Josephine, but I told Matthew about his son. I thought he should know."

I wish you hadn't done that appeared in the middle of my paper.

"Is Cooper worse?"

No, but we don't have test results back yet. You've upset Matthew unnecessarily, and there's nothing he can do for Cooper from there.

"My sentiments exactly. You need to get him home."

I wish I could. If I'd been able, I'd have brought him home as soon as I realized the gravity of Cooper's condition and let you and Vidocq solve this case on your own.

"Why can't you do that now? There must be a work-around for that whole 'must be a Wellingham' thing."

If there is, I haven't found it; and trust me, I've been diligently searching.

"Please keep trying, Josephine. They need to be together."

You think I don't know that?

"You're more aware of that fact than anyone. I'm concerned, that's all—and I realize you are as well."

If I come up with a solution, I'll let you know.

"Thank you."

I wasn't going to hold my breath. Still, Josephine wasn't the only one who could rack her brain for a solution.

CHAPTER 17

I didn't see Charles or Vidocq the next morning. Although that could have been because the jailer came to get me at daybreak, I was still afraid one or both of the men might be upset with me—Charles because I'd kept the information about Cooper from him for so long and Vidocq because I'd finally given Charles the information. I'd slept little, if any, and not only because the slab was so uncomfortable.

Reader, I could've gone off on a tangent about how much I longed for my comfy bed at home in North Carolina or even how much I missed that poufy feather bed at the Manette house and that what I truly missed was sleeping beside Charles on that bed, but I didn't want to bore you with an exposition about beds or a lack thereof. Nor did I feel I should tell you how terribly pitiful I felt being led out of my crummy cell knowing I might be walking to receive my death sentence having every man in my life totally ticked off at me. That information would only make us both weep big, honking teardrops.

Rather than hauling me into the courtroom, the jailer ushered me out into the courtyard.

"Since you're the cause of this duel, the judge thought you should be here to see it," he said.

"Wait, no. I don't want to—" I broke off when I saw Sydney and Sebastian standing back-to-back. It wasn't too late. "Stop this madness!"

Everyone except the duelers stopped what they were doing and gawked at me. The crowd grew quiet momentarily, watching to see if I'd somehow be successful in putting an end to the duel. Some of them glared as if they might shoot *me* if I knocked them out of their fun.

Using the silence to my advantage, I shouted, "Mr. Carton! Mr. Connor! I implore you both to apologize before this matter goes any further. I don't want there to be any blood shed by either of you, certainly not on my behalf!"

"Young lady, these men have made their decision." The judge might have been using a megaphone the way his voice carried, but I supposed he was merely used to projecting. He was perched on a chair situated in such a way as to provide the best view. "They and their seconds spoke prior to the commencement of these proceedings, which will now continue."

The judge's pronouncement brought a round of whoops and applause from the spectators. Someone did a drum roll. There was actually a drummer here. Would there be one at my execution if it came to that? I imagined there would be, and the notion made me feel a tad nauseous. I didn't want my death to be a source of entertainment for these people.

I searched the crowd for Charles and Vidocq. Although I didn't see Charles, I did catch a glimpse of Vidocq. He seemed to be as absorbed in the drama as the rest of the crowd.

The drum was silenced, and someone called out, "One!"

Sydney and Sebastian both took one pace forward.

Fifteen paces were counted out before the two men turned, raised their flintlock pistols, and fired.

At first, there was too much smoke from the gunshots to tell if anyone had been hit. But as the clouds from in front of each shooter dissipated, I could see blood spreading out on the left shoulder of Sebastian's tan waistcoat.

Covering my mouth to keep from screaming, I watched Sebastian crumple to the ground. A man with a black medical bag hurried over to him.

My eyes scanned from Sebastian's side of the lawn to Sydney's. Had Sydney been hit too? No. He was standing with Mr. Stryver, who I assumed was Sydney's second, and appeared to be reveling in his victory. But it wouldn't have mattered if Sydney had been shot or even killed. When the book reset, he would be back to his noble self. If Sebastian died, Connie would be dead. For real. No reset for her.

I caught a flash of white material at the side of my face. Turning, I found Charles handing me a handkerchief.

"Thank you." I pressed the silk cloth to my eyes but couldn't stem the tears streaming down my face. I gave up and stuffed the cloth into my pocket.

"I'm sorry," Charles said softly.

"I'm sorry too...f-for this...for last night...for everything." I nodded toward the spot where Sebastian lay. "W-will—? Is...is he—?"

"Vidocq is checking."

I nodded, grateful Charles had answered the question I couldn't bring myself to ask.

The jailer took my arm and started leading me away.

"Wait!" I tried to pull away from him, but his grip tightened on my arm.

"The show is over," he said. "Time to go back to your cell until the judge decides what to do about your trial." He jerked his chin in the direction of Sebastian. "That man won't be arguing against you anymore."

I whipped my head around to search the crowd for Vidocq before turning back toward Charles. He gave me a slight nod, which I took to mean he'd let me know something as soon as he could.

As the jailer walked me back into the building, I could hear the crowd being as raucous as if they'd just witnessed a sporting event that their team had won. How could they celebrate when Connie might be dead? I kept thinking that if she was, it was my fault.

Barely able to see through my tears, I stumbled.

"Aw, buck up, lass," the jailer said. "I imagine the prosecution will have to find another lawyer, get him familiar with your case and whatnot. All that will take time—and that's good for you."

"A man might've died at my expense. If so, his blood is on me."

"He might only be maimed. Either way, it was his decision to go through with the duel, and Carton bought you some time. You should thank the man."

At the moment, I didn't feel much like expressing any gratitude to Sydney Carton, but I didn't say so. The jailer deposited me in the cell, and I paced the floor and silently prayed that Connie would be all right.

WHEN AT LAST I heard footsteps in the hallway, I rushed toward the cell bars expecting it to be Charles or Vidocq with news of Connie. It was neither. It was Sydney Carton.

"Sydney, are you all right?"

"Not a scratch." He smiled warmly. "I heard you pacing, but there is no need for concern."

"And Seba—Mr. Connor? Will he be all right too?"

His smile became a grimace. "Your worry was for *him*? The man who would happily send you to the gallows?"

"I was afraid for both of you. I saw him bleeding from somewhere near his heart."

"Not near enough. Although I meant to kill him, the scoundrel lived."

"Did you duel with Mr. Connor to keep the trial from going forward?" I asked.

He lengthened his spine and fastened his hands to his lapels. "I challenged the man because he besmirched your honor. In how many more ways must I prove my love to you?"

"Sydney, I'm a married woman."

"Only because your father was weak. He should have called off the wedding as soon as he learned that you were about to marry an Evremonde. Charles Darnay deceived you both, and yet the wedding went forward as planned."

I gulped. "Wh-what have you done?"

"Obviously, not enough because you care nothing for me."

"Had you wanted to marry me, you should have asked for my hand."

The original Sydney Carton hadn't asked for Lucie's hand in marriage because he'd felt unworthy of her. I had no idea what was motivating this version of Sydney. Love? Maybe. But I wasn't sure that was the case. The original Sydney expressed his love by ultimately dying for Lucie's happiness. This one would certainly *kill* for her, but I doubted he would even consider dying.

A bead of sweat trickled down my spine. "Sydney, did

you kill my father?" The words emerged from my lips as little more than a whimper.

"Why would I do that? To hurt you? I've told you I'm in love with you and want nothing except your well-being."

"And for us to be together?"

"Yes, and that."

Charles and Vidocq came down the hall.

"Congratulations, Monsieur Carton," Vidocq said before he and Charles had reached my cell.

"Indeed," Charles said. "Good work."

"Thank you." Sydney took a step back from my cell. "I take it the judge has postponed the trial?"

"Yes." Charles looked at me. "Madame Grievous is furious."

"I can imagine," I said. "Is there any way Mr. Stryver could petition the court to let me be under house arrest until the new court date?" Was house arrest even a thing in the 1700s? I didn't know and didn't care. I just wanted out of this cell.

"He can try, but the outcome being favorable is not—" Vidocq struggled to find the English equivalent of what he wanted to say. "—*tres probable arriver.*"

"Not likely to happen," Charles translated.

"Great. I feel helpless in here. I can't assist in finding out who killed my father and prove my innocence. I'm unable to get a decent night's sleep. I'm worthless."

"We will concern ourselves with proving your innocence," Sydney said.

"You will be most pleased to know that Mr. Connor suffered only a wound to the shoulder," Vidocq said.

"I blame the wind," Sydney muttered.

"Is the trial postponed until the—" I nearly said *silver-fish.* "—the prosecution finds new representation? Or will they wait until Mr. Connor heals to resume the proceedings?"

"The judge hasn't ruled on that yet," Charles said. "We should know something by the end of the day."

"We will advise you *toute suite.*" Vidocq punctuated his words with a firm nod.

"Thank you." I sighed.

"And I'll speak with Mr. Stryver at once about preparing a motion to get you out of this horrible cell in the meantime," Sydney said.

"That motion would be this, *n'est-ce pas?*" Vidocq pantomimed unlocking the cell door and opening it with a flourish.

I laughed.

Sydney glared at him. "You take nothing seriously, do you, Monsieur Vidocq?"

"*Au contraire,* there are many things about which I am most solemn."

"I'll take my leave, gentlemen." Sydney bowed to me. "I pray I return soon with welcome news of your impending release."

"She should not hold the breath," Vidocq murmured.

Sydney stopped, stiffened, but apparently decided it

A TALE OF TWO ENEMIES

was beneath him to respond. He continued striding down the hall.

"Is he gone?" I mouthed to Charles a moment later.

Charles walked down the hall to check and returned to say, "He's gone. Also, I bribed the judge to make sure we have fifteen minutes uninterrupted."

"Thanks." I wiped my damp palms down the sides of my dress.

"*Merci* from me as well." Vidocq grinned. "I delight in being part of the intrigue."

"As I've already told you, Connie will be fine," Charles said. "I do imagine that the silverfish will expel her from Literatia immediately and will never hire her again."

"I hope the expulsion has already taken place. I'd like to think she's in the hands of modern medical professionals by now." I blew out a breath. "But, guys, I think Sydney Carton might've killed my father."

Neither of them expressed as much surprise as I'd thought they might, and they patiently allowed me to make my case without interruption.

"On the day of the wedding, Sydney thought I came back to the house because I was regretting my decision. He thought I was going to speak with my father about annulling the marriage. Also, he knew Charles confessed to Dr. Manette prior to the wedding that he'd been born an Evremonde. He's declared his love for me more than once and has admitted to trying to kill Connie." Nodding toward Vidocq, I added. "You were right—my calling Sebastian 'Connie' infuriated Sydney. I believe he thought the two of us either were or had been lovers and that his mistaken assumption was the real reason he challenged Sebastian to a duel."

"I'll grant you that," Charles said, "but why would Sydney kill Dr. Manette? And if he did, why didn't he confess to keep you from being arrested?"

"I don't think he's that gallant. In his perfect world, I would be set free, Charles would either be convicted of Dr. Manette's murder or sent to the guillotine for being a member of the French aristocracy, and Sydney and I could live happily ever after."

"Ah, you believe Sydney Carton will attempt to plant the evidence implicating Charles in your father's murder, *ma petite?*"

"I do. He might have even tried already and been thwarted by the silverfish." I half smiled. "Sydney is working against the silverfish and doesn't even know it. I wonder what great things could happen if all the characters were aware of the silverfish and worked together to get the story back on track and eradicate them."

Charles laughed. "My darling, you are absolutely brilliant. Come on, Vidocq. We've got work to do."

Vidocq spread his hands, shrugged, and trailed down the hall behind Charles. I desperately wished I was going with them.

CHAPTER 18

I spent much of the day wondering whether Mr. Stryver could get me moved from this dank, dingy cell into house arrest. Then late that afternoon, the jailer came and—much like Vidocq had demonstrated—unlocked the door and flung it open.

"Mrs. Darnay, you are free to go."

"How? Am I under house arrest now?"

The man looked confused but said, "Someone else confessed to the murder of Alexandre Manette."

"Who?" Now I was the one bewildered. If someone else had confessed to the murder, why hadn't the book reset? Why was I still here in *A Tale of Two Cities*? Had Josephine been able to extricate Charles—or, rather, Matthew—instead?

"Your husband," the jailer said.

"Charles confessed to killing my father?" I asked. "But, why? He's innocent. I'm sure of it. We both are."

"One thing I've learned in my line of work, lass, is that you can't be sure of anyone or anything. I believe one of your friends is waiting to take you home."

"May I see my husband first?" This must be part of the plan Charles and Vidocq had left to work on yesterday.

The jailer took me to a cell where Charles was standing with his back to the bars.

"Charles," I said softly.

He kept his back to us. "Give us a moment of privacy, won't you, my good man?"

"Five minutes." The jailer left me alone in front of the cell.

Charles turned. Only it wasn't Charles. It was Sydney Carton. My eyes widened, and my mouth opened.

Before I could speak, Sydney put a finger to his lips.

"But—" I began.

Shaking his head vehemently, he walked closer to the bars and spoke to me quietly. "It will all become clear soon. Or so I am told. I know there are forces at work in our lives that I don't understand—evil forces that will turn on one of their own for no logical reason."

"I have no idea what's going on," I whispered, "but I know you had to have taken a monumental leap of faith to be here. Do you know who I am?"

"I know who you are not." He smiled softly. "Much of what our friends told me baffled me, but I feel they are good men, and I trust them."

I made no attempt to hold back the tears that welled

up. "You're the man I knew all along you were. May I kiss your cheek?"

"You may." He angled his head so I could briefly kiss his stubbly cheek.

"On behalf of me, the real Lucie, and the people all over the world who you're helping by assisting us, thank you. Thank you from the bottom of my heart."

"It is a far, far better thing that I do, than I have ever done," he said.

Oh, Reader, hearing Sydney Carton—the Sydney Carton —speak those famous words to me was my undoing. I began to sob so loudly that I was sure I could be heard throughout the entire jail.

"It will be all right, love," Sydney said. "Seeing you like this breaks my heart."

I couldn't even speak. It was as if I was a teenager again, reading the words Sydney had just spoken for the first time, picturing him there at the guillotine prepared to die for love. This time, he'd said those words to me personally, and it made me realize that Sydney Carton was *real*.

Of course, I understood Sydney Carton was a fictional character, but when I'd initially read *A Tale of Two Cities*, he'd become so alive to me. Moments ago, I'd pressed my lips to his face, and he'd been as real as anyone else in Literatia, including me. I finally understood what it was we were truly fighting for in the world of Literatia. Sure, we were keeping the silverfish from destroying great works of literature, but it was the *char-*

acters we were truly saving. My mind began racing through all the wonderful characters I'd met over the years in books. I didn't want to lose them.

"I don't want to lose you," I said to Sydney, as my sobs subsided.

"You won't." He gave me a brave smile, which he dropped when the jailer started down the hall.

"Time's up, folks. Come along, Mrs. Darnay."

I nodded, well aware of the fact that I had to pull myself together and work with Charles and Vidocq to perform my part of the plan—whatever that was. With one last look over my shoulder at Sydney, I allowed the jailer to usher me out to the lobby where Vidocq was waiting.

"Ah, what a shock you have had, Mrs. Darnay," he said. "I have a carriage waiting to take us to your home." He took my arm and escorted me outside. Looking all around to make sure no one was listening, he said, "*Tres bon* with the wailing, *ma petite*. I truly believed your heart was breaking, and I was nearly moved to tears myself."

"The real Sydney hadn't been corrupted as much as we'd thought," I said.

"*Oui*. Otherwise, our plan would have been the failure." He helped me into the carriage, sat across from me, and shut the door. "You knew at once he was not Charles?"

"Not immediately because he had his back to me. I realized it as soon as he faced me." I took the silk handkerchief Charles had given me the day before from my pocket and wiped my eyes. "Are you going to fill me in on the plan?"

"Not yet. Charles and I prefer to do that together." He gestured toward the handkerchief. "Do not put that away just yet, however, because I have to tell you distressing news. It is *tres horrible*, but it is what convinced Sydney to trust us and to believe that there are dark forces at work in this world."

I twisted the handkerchief in my hands and took a deep breath. "Tell me."

"Charles and I, we had attempted to persuade Sydney to go along with our plan. As you perhaps can imagine, the man believed us to be insane, and he left us. But later he returned to us with news from Mr. Stryver that changed his mind."

"Vidocq, tell me the horrible thing."

"I am working up to it. Mr. Stryver received a note from the judge saying your case was being postponed until the prosecution had secured a new lawyer because theirs had died in a duel that morning."

"That's a lie. Everyone said Sebastian Connor would be okay. Even if he'd had to wait to get medical attention—"

"The doctor who attended the duel was not a silverfish, *ma petite*. He removed the lead ball from Sebastian Connor's shoulder and sewed up the wound," he said. "Many people survived gunshots in the 1700s, you know."

"Of course. I'm sorry. I never intended to insult—" I

broke off as the news finally sunk in. "Are you saying Connie is dead? Or are you telling me the silverfish sent her back home and claimed their lawyer was dead to stall for time or something?"

"Sebastian Connor—your friend, Connie—is dead. The judge saw the body." Vidocq leaned forward and took my hand.

"But maybe Connie was faking for the judge's benefit. You know, she could have been lying really still with her eyes closed. Right?"

"*Non, ma petite.* A friend of Mr. Carton's who accompanied the judge to see the body reported that Sebastian Connor had been stabbed through the heart."

"The judge witnessed the duel!"

"Not so loud, *s'il te plait,*" Vidocq cautioned.

"Sorry." I lowered my voice. "But the judge knows fully well that Sebastian Connor didn't die in that duel. He watched the entire thing and saw each man fire one shot. They didn't swordfight afterwards."

"*Oui,* that's true."

"Then why is he allowing the silverfish to get away with murdering Sebastian Connor?" I asked.

"I have no answer for that other than corruption."

I threw my head back against the seat and gazed up at the ceiling of the carriage. Connie was dead. In Literaia. At home. Yes, I was sad about it; but more than that, I was angry. Why would the silverfish kill someone they'd brought into the book? Couldn't they have simply let her go if they didn't need her anymore? And why would the judge turn a blind eye to what they'd done? Was he a silverfish himself?

We arrived at the Manette house, and Vidocq helped me alight from the carriage. Charles was standing on the stoop.

"Ah, look, Mrs. Darnay," Vidocq's voice boomed. "It's Mr. Carton!"

As if I hadn't gotten the memo.

"Yes." Charles stepped forward. "I hope you will forgive my intrusion at such a distressing time for you, but I felt we should discuss some legal matters."

I nodded and preceded both Charles and Vidocq into the house. After asking the maid to bring in some tea, I went into the salon and sat on the sofa. Charles stood by the fireplace, and Vidocq sat on the armchair. None of us spoke until after the maid had brought the tea and left again.

I filled the three cups and stirred a spoonful of sugar into mine.

"Are you all right?" Charles asked, sitting beside me on the sofa.

"I'm not sure."

We all spoke in hushed voices.

Vidocq moved the armchair closer to the table. "I told her about Sebastian Connor on the way here."

"And...the other?" Charles asked.

"He didn't have to tell me. The moment I saw *his* face, I knew." I realized we weren't saying Sydney's name in case any of the silverfish in the house were listening.

They'd been known to send a single silverfish from its host to do reconnaissance for them, so it paid to take precautions. "So, what's going on?"

"As I told you already, *the other party* wouldn't agree to participate in our subterfuge until Sebastian Connor turned up dead," Vidocq said.

"Killed at the hand of Madame Grievous if I had to place a bet." I took a drink of the tea, welcoming the way it warmed me as I swallowed. "How did he—the other party—know it wasn't one of you who'd had Connie murdered?"

"We didn't believe she was actually dead," Charles said. "We told the other party that we believed the dark forces determined to destroy this nation had sent Sebastian Connor away and had announced his death in order to damage Mr. Carton's reputation with the court."

"Vidocq said a friend of Mr. Carton's had seen her... er, him."

Charles put his arm around me. "I'm sorry for your loss."

"She warned me of the risk I was taking when I was willing to stand trial for the murder of Dr. Manette. She had to know she was as much in danger as I was, but Connie always did seem to feel as if the rules didn't apply where she was concerned." I directed my gaze to Charles' face. "Why did the silverfish kill her? Why not merely send her away? There was no need to stab her to death."

"I'm inclined to believe Madame Grievous murdered Connie in a rage," he said. "Connie was hired and brought into this book because of her connection to you. She knew that herself. And she failed in the task the silverfish set before her."

"But she didn't get a chance to fail," I said. "The duel prevented her from carrying out the trial."

"The trial was not why she was hired, *ma petite*." Vidocq refilled his teacup. "She was meant to convince you to take the deal. And in that regard, she failed."

I ran a hand over my face. "Still, she could have convicted me at trial. She was working with a stacked deck."

"It doesn't matter. Their goal was to get rid of us both. Since the silverfish know *A Tale of Two Cities* involves two men who love the same woman," Charles, "Madame Grievous wasn't surprised when Charles Darnay confessed to the crime to absolve his wife."

"About that," I said. "Where do we go from here?"

"Vidocq will remain here as your guest and the faithful relative of Charles Darnay," Charles said.

"I will be most convincing, as I am positive neither my relative nor his beloved wife committed this atrocity."

I couldn't help but smile at Vidocq's fervor. "How could anyone ever doubt you?"

"I will be going to my home, of course," Charles said, fishing keys I assumed were to Sydney Carton's house from his pocket. "Meanwhile, the four of us will determine who actually killed Dr. Manette as soon as possible to reset the book."

"I understand that Connie's—well, Sebastian Connor's—death convinced the other party that dark forces are at work here," I said. "Did you tell him he's a character in a book?"

"No. We told him we are spies working to keep an elite French faction from starting a war between our two countries," Charles said. "We mentioned that Dr. Manette was also a spy helping us to keep peace and that once we find the culprit who slayed him and reclaim vital information, everything will go back to normal."

"That was pretty brilliant." I rested my head against Charles' shoulder.

"Thanks. But here is the most important thing, you must be extra vigilant. Always keep your door locked and never leave this house without Vidocq or me by your side."

"I vow not to let you out of my sight, *ma petite*. Except to sleep. And I will even stand guard at the bedside, if necessary."

"It isn't," I put in quickly, "but I appreciate the offer." Having Vidocq watch me sleep could be almost as unnerving as having to sleep with one eye open to guard against the silverfish. "How will we up our game with regard to the investigation?"

"This is where it might get a little dicey for you." Charles lifted my chin to look into my eyes. "With your husband in jail and your father gone, you'll now turn back to your old nanny for comfort."

I sat up and placed my empty teacup on the tray. "Am I feeding her false information, or what?"

"Yes, but you'll also be manipulating the conversation to see what she might let slip. As a lesser silverfish, she isn't as powerful as someone like Madame Grievous. Press her for more information about the day Dr. Manette died."

"And even if you may appear to be speaking with Miss Pross privately, I will always be near because we are as yet unsure whether or not she murdered Dr. Manette herself." Vidocq rubbed his chin. "What shall be our code word which upon hearing I shall come bursting in?"

"How about *incorrigible*?" I grinned. "That isn't a word I'd normally use when speaking with Miss Pross, and I find myself constantly applying it to you."

"*Tres bien*. If I hear you utter the word *incorrigible*, I shall rush to save you at once."

"I appreciate it."

Charles stood. "I should leave now. Lingering here might draw suspicion. Tomorrow we will meet in town. Vidocq and I have it arranged already."

"Will you be okay?" I also stood.

"Yes. I am no threat to the silverfish." He winked.

I quickly kissed him. "Don't be arrogant. None of us should ever let our guard down."

Vidocq and I walked Charles out of the salon and to the front door.

"Thank you again for coming, Mr. Carton," I said, in a

normal tone of voice. "I truly appreciate your help in getting this mess sorted out."

"I'm happy to be of assistance." He bowed slightly—very Sydney like, I thought—and left.

How I hated to see him go. I knew he was better equipped to take on a new identity here in Literatia than I would be, but still, he was going it alone. At least, I had Vidocq here to assist me.

As if reading my thoughts, Vidocq patted my shoulder. "Everything will be fine, *madame.*"

I prayed he was right; but as the two of us returned to the salon, I couldn't keep my thoughts from turning back to Connie.

CHAPTER 19

I lay awake most of the night. Not only was I afraid the silverfish would try to get into my room, I had Connie on my mind.

What would her family think? Would they believe she'd gone missing, been kidnapped, or had some sort of accident and been unable to call for help? I recalled how close Connie had been to her family when we were in college together. They'd know—her mother, in particular —that Connie would never willingly abandon them.

I even thought about Connie's cat, Sebastian. Connie would call to talk with her mom and to check on that cat once a day from our freshman year on until graduation.

Had time not moved so much more quickly in Literatia than in our world, I'd have considered going to visit Connie's parents after this book had reset—provided I made it home myself. But what would I even say? What *could* I say?

The way Cooper had explained it to me after my first foray into Literatia, there were 1440 minutes in a day in our world. In Literatia, time was two percent of that. A person could be in Literatia an entire day, but that would translate to only half an hour in our world.

Besides, I had no intention of leaving Literatia when *A Tale of Two Cities* reset. I'd even thought of a way for Josephine to help me with that. But first things first.

I got up and put on my shoes and the black mourning dress. Just because Charles was sleeping elsewhere didn't mean I wasn't going to be almost fully dressed when I went to bed. With the stakes having been raised even higher than they already were, I had to be ready for anything.

After brushing my hair and pinning it up, I left my room. Having no idea what time it was, I tiptoed to Vidocq's room and tapped softly on the door, not wanting to disturb him if he was still asleep.

He swung open the door so quickly that I jumped back in alarm.

"What is happening?" he asked. "I am not missing anything?"

"No. I merely wanted to ask if you'd slept well and if you'd like to go with me to rustle up some breakfast."

"I did not sleep well, *ma petite*, and by all means, let us rustle."

As we descended the stairs, I heard someone moving around in the kitchen. It was the cook.

"Breakfast is almost ready, madam. You and Mister

Vidocq sit down in the dining room, and I'll bring your food in to you soon."

"Thank you," I said. "If you see Miss Pross, would you please ask her to join us?"

Vidocq and I went into the dining room. I sat at the head of the table where Charles would normally sit, and Vidocq sat on my left where he could face the door.

"After breakfast, we will go and visit Charles, *n'est-ce pas?*"

"Yes. I'll take him some food." I knew we were speaking of Sydney. "I know how bad that jail food is."

Miss Pross came into the dining room but didn't sit. "Cook said you wished to see me."

It took all the acting skills I possessed to give the silverfish Miss Pross a warm smile. "I hoped you'd join Monsieur Vidocq and me for breakfast. It feels as if we haven't had a meal together in ages."

The small, elderly woman pulled out the chair to my right and sat. "I'm sorry I didn't visit you at the jail. I couldn't stand to see you there."

"It's all right, dear." Gritting my teeth, I patted her gnarled hand and hoped no silverfish would crawl onto me. I drew back my hand and surreptitiously wiped it on my skirt.

"I understand it was you who sounded the alarm when Dr. Manette was struck down," Vidocq said.

"Yes, and I've been over that day countless times. I do not wish to speak of it anymore."

"Indulge me please." Vidocq placed a hand over his

heart. "Monsieur Darnay is my kinsman. I am as sure of his innocence as I am that the sun will rise tomorrow. Won't you please give me a full account of your day, Miss Pross?"

"Oh, please do," I said. "I'd love to hear all about that day from your perspective. It was both the happiest and the saddest day of my life."

I felt Vidocq and I were working well together, especially since we hadn't discussed anything about how we'd manage this conversation beforehand.

"Very well." Miss Pross primly folded her hands. "I was ever so excited when I woke up that morning. I could hardly wait to help you get ready for the wedding. You were the most beautiful bride I'd ever seen, as I knew you would be."

"I fully believe that and regret I was unable to attend the wedding," Vidocq said. "Alas, business in France detained me."

Giving him a look begging him not to interrupt, I attempted to get Miss Pross talking again. "How did Father seem to you? Did he appear to be concerned about my marriage to Charles?"

"I don't believe so. No more than any father whose only daughter was about to be wed."

"That's good to know." I exchanged glances with Vidocq. If Miss Pross should testify to the contrary at the trial, then we could both dispute her statement. "Did he have any visitors that you know of before the wedding?"

"Only Mr. Lorry." Miss Pross frowned slightly. "That

wasn't unusual, of course. Mr. Lorry was here most days as he and your father were fast friends, you know. But they were having a serious discussion about money that morning."

"Money?" I gave a little gasp. "We aren't in dire financial straits, are we?"

"I would not be inclined to believe so, although you should discuss those matters pertaining to household finances with the people of Tellson's if you feel concerned," she said. "What I overheard was Mr. Lorry asking Dr. Manette for a loan, but your father refused. He said he could no longer bail Mr. Lorry out of trouble."

"And what was Mr. Lorry's response to that?" Vidocq asked.

Miss Pross put her nose in the air. "I did not wait around in the hallway to hear, *monsieur*, as I am no eavesdropper."

"Of course, you aren't." I gave her a reassuring nod but was thinking, *oh, yes, you absolutely are.* "After Monsieur Vidocq and I visit Charles at the jail this morning, we will go to Tellson's Bank to visit Mr. Lorry and make sure there are adequate funds in our account. I don't know what might become of me if I were forced to sell our home and leave London."

"That's not supposed to happen," Miss Pross said.

Raising my eyebrows, I said, "None of this was *supposed* to happen, was it?"

"No. That's..." She gulped. "That's what I meant. How could Fate be so cruel as to deal you another blow?"

VIDOCQ and I were in the carriage on our way to the jail to see Sydney-slash-Charles before I brought up the conversation we'd had with Miss Pross at breakfast.

"That bit Miss Pross said about my selling the house and leaving London was *not supposed* to happen is still cartwheeling around in my brain," I told him. "After we visit the jail, we should go straight to Tellson's and talk with Mr. Lorry. We'll say I want to ascertain whether or not I have the money to mount an adequate legal defense for my husband."

"Agreed. You must say, however, that you are of the opinion that Mr. Stryver is a fine man but that perhaps he is not knowledgeable enough in trials of murder to adequately represent Charles. Lucie Manette would be respectful and placid, not one to march into Mr. Lorry's office and say that Mr. Stryver is a lousy lawyer."

"You're absolutely right. I'll be careful with my phrasing."

He grinned. "*Merci.* As we all know, a man is most often murdered either out of anger, greed, or lust. No offense to Dr. Manette, but I am confident we can eliminate the lust."

"Yeah, me too. And if we seem to be ready to liquidate Dr. Manette's money, it shouldn't take long for us to find out if greed was the motive. Mr. Stryver was ever so eager to get his fee for preparing Dr. Manette's will."

"We should inquire about the contents of the will,"

Vidocq said. "The person who killed Dr. Manette was eager to frame his daughter for the murder."

"But I thought that was the silverfishes' doing." I frowned. "Wasn't it?"

"Madame Grievous—a major silverfish—sent her envoy to offer you a deal in which she could testify either for you or against you. And the silverfish inserted the prosecutor of their choice into the trial." He flipped his palms. "That does not mean they put your brooch in Dr. Manette's clasped hand, only that they took advantage of the situation."

"So, the silverfish offered to give damning testimony against me in order to *help* the killer?" I asked.

"No, they wanted only to help themselves. By—as I once heard you say it—stacking the deck of cards against you, they made you feel as if you were in an unwinnable situation."

What Vidocq was saying finally clicked with me. "It's a catch-22."

"I do not know how many were involved in trying to catch you, but that is not the point. The point is the silverfish tried to take advantage of your fear and convince you to turn your back on Literatia and those you care for." He shook his fist. "But they failed to consider the bravery of *ma petite!*"

I laughed. "I don't know about that. The whole experience was terrifying."

"*Oui,* but soon we will make things right."

"I hope so."

CHAPTER 20

Sydney was as grateful for the food I'd brought as I had been with the treats Charles and Vidocq had delivered to me. He had devoured one piece of bread with jam and had started on another when I finally decided that if we were going to get anything accomplished today, I'd better speak.

"Poor Charles. Haven't they fed you at all since they brought you here?"

"Nothing this good," he said. "Have you made any progress on our case yet?"

"Not much, but we are diligently seeking answers," Vidocq said. "Thinking the murder might have been motivated by material gain, I thought we should take a look at Dr. Manette's will today. Mr. Stryver will have a copy of it, *non?*"

Sydney looked at me. "You don't have your father's will, Lucie?"

"I haven't checked Father's study yet. I thought that since I'm going to Tellson's Bank today to get a better idea of our financial situation, I could check with Mr. Stryver while I'm out, provided he has time to see me."

"There's no need to make a trip to Stryver's office about the will if you're going to Tellson's." Sydney wiped some jam from the corner of his mouth with his thumb. "Jarvis Lorry is the executor of your father's estate. He's sure to have a copy of the will."

"Mr. Lorry is the executor, you say? That's of great interest," Vidocq said.

I could practically see the wheels turning in my friend's head. "You think—"

"Tut-tut." He raised a hand to silence me. "Let us not bore your husband with talk of business. He has much on his mind already. He is in need of our assurances, *non?*"

"Yes, of course." I smiled at Sydney. "Charles, my love, we have no doubt you're innocent of this crime, and I'm going to do whatever it takes to save you. Even if it means spending every cent we have. We can always start over and build a life somewhere new."

"*Oui,* the two of you shall live with me, if necessary. That is what the family is for, *n'est-ce pas?*"

"What a generous offer, Vidocq," Sydney said. "Isn't it, darling?"

"It is. Meeting Vidocq makes me regret that I haven't met more members of your family." I realized the faux pas I'd made as soon as I'd said it. Lucie hadn't met any of

Charles' family because he'd denounced the name Evremonde and all the tyranny that went with it.

Sydney seemed to have understood what I'd done,
and he covered for me beautifully. "Vidocq is the one
bright spot in my family tree, my love. Once you've met
him, you've met the best."

"*Merci.*" Vidocq inclined his head.

I breathed a sigh of relief. Anyone spying for Madame
Grievous would have learned only what we wanted the
silverfish to know during this visit; in particular, that we
were planning on liquidating Dr. Manette's assets.

As soon as the carriage pulled away from the jail, I let
out a long breath. "Dang. I thought I'd blown it back
there."

"You blew on nothing. The visit went well. Should the
jailer have been spying for Madame Grievous, which we
are almost positive he was, then she will soon know that
you are willing to do whatever it takes to free Charles—
even that which is not supposed to happen."

"I'm glad you're able to catch on to my idioms so
well," I said with a smile. "Also, we gained some valuable
information from Sydney. We now know Jarvis Lorry is
the executor of Dr. Manette's estate."

By the time we'd arrived at Tellson's Bank and Vidocq
had helped me down from the carriage, I was already
playing the part of the distraught bride. Vidocq ushered

me inside and told a clerk that he and I needed an audience with Mr. Lorry at once.

Mr. Lorry came out and escorted us to his office. He'd never met Vidocq.

"Thank you for meeting with us," Mr. Lorry," I said. "This gentleman is Eugene Francois Vidocq, a kinsman of my husband. Monsieur Vidocq, this is Jarvis Lorry, one of my father's oldest and dearest friends."

The two men exchanged pleasantries, and then I was ready to get down to business.

"Mr. Lorry, I need to be advised as to how much money Father left me in his accounts."

The old man's eyebrows shot up. "Whatever for? Don't you have everything you need?"

"For now." I did my best to appear indecisive. "I'm sorry to say this—and please, sir, do not repeat what I am saying to you in confidence—but I fear Mr. Stryver isn't competent to argue a trial of the magnitude my husband now faces. I intend to spend every cent I have if necessary to ensure Charles is set free. I know he'd never harm my father and that he's innocent. As am I."

"Now, now, Miss Lucie, you have gone and gotten yourself all agitated." Mr. Lorry leaned forward, placed his elbows on his desk, and steepled his fingers. "Mr. Stryver will do a fine job representing Charles."

"Nevertheless, I'd like to see Father's will and the ledger showing the amount of money in his—I mean, *our* —account."

"The will?" Mr. Lorry screwed up his face. "Why

would a delicate lady such as yourself wish to see your father's will? Trust that you were well provided for."

"I do believe that my father made every allowance for my future, but I would still like to read the document for myself."

Mr. Lorry didn't move.

"You *are* the executor of my father's will, are you not?" I asked.

"I am." He put his arms down, but he still made no effort to stand.

"I truly appreciate your gathering the information I've requested." I gave him a frigid smile.

At last, he stood and left the office, shutting the door behind him.

Sinking down in my chair, I whispered to Vidocq, "I hate confrontation."

"Perhaps. But you are ever so good at it, *ma petite*."

I straightened when I heard footsteps in the hall, hoping I'd be able to maintain my façade of composure for a little bit longer.

Mr. Lorry entered the office and returned to his chair behind the desk. "I am still at a loss to understand why you no longer trust me to handle your affairs."

"My request for knowledge has nothing to do with my confidence in you, Mr. Lorry. Naturally, I have the utmost assurance that you will look out for me."

Reader, I nearly choked on that lie. His behavior had wrung out any drop of faith I might've ever had in the man. Sure, he could've been merely behaving as a typical 18th

Century man who thought he should be able to pat me on the head and send me on my way, But he'd soon realize he wasn't dealing with a typical 18th Century woman.

"Madame Darnay seeks only the confirmation that all is well and that she will be able to provide Charles with the finest legal team available," Vidocq said.

"I understand, but I can't imagine why Miss Lucie has lost hope in Mr. Stryver."

My impatience got the best of me. "I've lost hope in the man because I am sitting here in your office rather than in a filthy jail cell with no thanks to Mr. Stryver whatsoever." I lifted my chin. "The only reason I was released is because my beloved husband confessed to a crime he did not commit in order to have me set free. All Mr. Stryver seemed to care about immediately following my father's death was receiving payment for the will he'd drafted. I can't think this trial is anything more than another opportunity to earn a fee. Now, please, Mr. Lorry, delay no longer in allowing me access to my financial information."

With a scowl, Mr. Lorry slid both the ledger—open to my father's account—and the will across the desk. I took a look at the bottom line on the bank account and saw that Dr. Manette had been better off than I'd expected him to be.

I took more time with the will, but there were no surprises there. Dr. Manette had left everything to his only child, Lucie. Should Lucie marry and have children, and should Dr. Manette outlive his daughter, his estate would be divided among Lucie's children. And yadda, yadda. There was no provision for anyone outside the family to inherit.

Glancing up, I saw that Mr. Lorry was watching me intently.

Unless.

I lowered my eyes back to the will. It wasn't specifically spelled out in the document before me, but I knew that should the sole beneficiary—Lucie Manette—be convicted of murdering the testator, the estate would pass to the executor—Jarvis Lorry. That's why I had been framed.

Pushing the documents back across the desk, I stood. "Thank you for your time, Mr. Lorry. I feel more secure now that I've seen the documents."

Nope, Reader, I did not feel secure at all. I felt scared. Maybe not pee myself scared, but close. Remembering what Miss Pross had said about the argument between Mr. Lorry and Dr. Manette made me realize I was the only thing standing between a desperate man and a pile of money.

WHEN VIDOCQ and I picked up Charles a few minutes later, I threw my arms around him as soon as the carriage door was closed.

Charles cradled my head against his chest. "Sweetheart, you're trembling. What's happened?"

Vidocq answered for me. "We are almost certain we just met with Dr. Manette's killer, Jarvis Lorry."

"It's not only the silverfish who want me dead." My words were muffled, as I was speaking into Charles' chest, but I didn't care enough to raise my head. "I wouldn't be surprised if Lorry didn't hire a killer to get rid of me too."

"If he hasn't, then we should introduce him to one."

Charles' words did make me lift up my head and look at him as if he were insane. "Are you insane? You want to set Jarvis Lorry up with someone willing to kill me?"

Vidocq leaned forward in his seat. "*Bien sur!* Of course! You are a genius, Charles. I will offer to kill Lucie for half the money in the bank account. The house and other contents of the will shall be his to do with as he sees fit."

"That's smart," I said, finally catching on. "As far as Mr. Lorry knows, you and I only met a few days ago. You can pretend to be down on your luck, staying with the Darnays only because you're going from one relation to the next until you're thrown out and forced to find another relative to mooch off of." I smiled. "You can really sell this, Vidocq. I'm sure you can."

"I am also sure I will sell it." He grinned. "It will be most fun to play the blackguard."

"If Mr. Lorry truly is our murderer, will the book reset automatically?" I asked. "It didn't in *Jane Eyre*."

"We shall see," Charles said. "Sometimes the transformation is immediate, and at other times, there is a delay.

It depends on how much the original manuscript has been corrupted."

"And *A Tale of Two Cities* has been corrupted a lot." I sighed and rested my head against Charles' chest again. "That means the silverfish will try to kill us both before the book resets."

"We will not allow that to happen, *ma petite.*"

Charles tilted my head up with his index finger. "No, darling, we will not." He gently kissed my lips.

I nodded and put my head back down. As Charles and Vidocq discussed their plan for having Jarvis Lorry confess to having killed Dr. Manette, my mind was ruminating on my next steps in getting Charles home.

CHAPTER 21

At the Manette house, I told Vidocq I needed to lie down for a few minutes.

"You'll be all right on your own for a while, won't you, Monsieur Vidocq?"

He gave me a pointed look. "*Oui.* I must return to town and take care of some personal business. Rest well."

In the carriage, he and I had decided this course of action—that I'd say I was tired, go upstairs to my room, lock the door, and stay there until Vidocq returned from offering himself as a hired assassin to Jarvis Lorry.

"I will. Thank you."

Vidocq squinted at me, and I smiled. He could tell I was planning something, but he had no clue as to what it was. I'd kept my plot completely secret because I had no idea if it would even work.

Were we not here in plain sight of any silverfish who might be walking around inside or outside of the house,

I'd have hugged Vidocq. I hoped I'd see him again, only not as Lucie Manette.

I turned and ascended the stairs. Vidocq remained where he was until he'd watched me get to the top. I gave him a wink before going into my room and closing the door.

Both Vidocq and Charles had been concerned about leaving me unprotected with the silverfish and possibly even with another killer already hired by Jarvis Lorry. Charles had even offered to accompany me home as Sydney, but I said that would look too suspicious. Now, as I locked the door behind me, I decided that if Josephine did as I asked, there was no need for me to be concerned about either the silverfish or any hired killer.

I immediately got a piece of paper and the shard of charcoal Vidocq had procured for me when I was in jail. I wrote, "Josephine, I desperately need your help. Are you there?"

I'm here.

"Can you get me out of this book and immediately put me back in as Sydney Carton?"

She didn't answer.

Instead, I felt myself grow faint, and tightly closed my eyes. When I opened them, I was in the Smithmore Manor library. Josephine was standing in front of me.

I smiled and let out a sigh of relief.

"We don't have much time," she said.

Taking the wedding ring from my finger, I pressed it into her hand. "Keep this safe for me."

"You're sure about this?"

"Positive." I didn't even have time to ask about Cooper. Things were moving at breakneck speed, and I had to get back into the book before it reset.

I felt a whooshing that made me lightheaded once again. I blinked several times, and when my eyes adjusted, I was standing in the jail cell.

Reader, it was all I could do not to do a fist pump. Instead, I acted like a man condemned and went over to sit on the stone slab.

I held my hands out and examined them. Manly hands. Sydney Carton's hands. I nearly giggled, I was so pleased with myself. I'd done it. I thought.

When I heard footsteps in the hallway, I put my hands down and affected an expression of boredom.

Madame Grievous stopped outside my cell and glared at me.

I didn't stand. I merely gazed back at her from where I sat and tried with everything in me not to allow my expression to change. I had to remain strong.

"I suppose you think you've won," she said.

"Why is that?"

"Because you and your team of interlopers managed to solve the murder of Alexandre Manette and save another manuscript."

I concentrated on pressing my tongue to the roof of my mouth so I could hold onto my composed expression. Inside, I was jumping up and down with joy. We had won.

Madame Grievous continued talking. "But even though you saved the book, you failed to save your precious Gia."

My jaw dropped. I was genuinely surprised. "What?"

She laughed. "Your man, Vidocq, left her alone when he went to coerce a confession out of Jarvis Lorry. He left *Lucie* resting in her room with the door locked, but when she heard poor Miss Pross fall down the stairs, she rushed to the old lady's aid." She scoffed. "Idiot. Miss Pross faked the falling noises and stabbed your lady friend as soon as she opened the door. And you weren't there to save her."

I lowered my head and shielded my face with my hands. I needed to think, and the perceptive Madame Grievous shouldn't be watching my face as I processed this new information. Poor Lucie Manette. She'd come back into her character just in time to be murdered by someone she'd cherished all her life.

Letting out another cackle, Madame Grievous said, "I'll leave you alone in your misery. Be warned that your time is coming."

I was relieved to hear her footsteps echoing back down the hallway, but I didn't take my hands away from my face. The silverfish thought they had killed me, and that was good. On the other hand, Vidocq and Charles likely believed me to be dead too. I wanted to let them know I was all right, but I couldn't take the risk. Charles would know soon enough—he might even know now if Josephine had extracted him from the book already. But I didn't want Vidocq to think I was either one, dead, or two, stupid enough to fall for silverfish trickery.

Fortunately, I didn't have to wait long to learn what Vidocq thought. He arrived only minutes after Madame Grievous departed.

Upon lifting my head and seeing him, I broke into a wide smile and hurried over to the bars. "I'm happy to see you."

He shook his finger at me. "I knew you were up to the something, *ma petite*," he whispered. "But do not look so delighted. I've come to inform you of your wife's demise."

"I already know. Madame Grievous came to gloat." I hesitated. "Is he gone?"

"Not yet."

"Does he *know*?"

Vidocq nodded. "I told him before coming to see you. I said to him, 'Vidocq knew she was up to the something, *mon ami*. It is almost impossible to fool Vidocq."

"I'm aware, and I was counting on it."

"Oh, go and pretend to be sad until your next assignment. He will visit you before he leaves if it is possible."

I reached between the bars and patted Vidocq's arm. "I hope we meet again soon."

"I have it on good authority that we will." He tipped his hat and walked away.

I went back to the stone slab and sat with my back to the bars, not sure I could look sad if my life depended on it—which it still might.

As I waited for whatever would come next, I pondered what that something might be. There had been several books on the watch list before I'd been sent into *A Tale of Two Cities*. Would it be one of those or would there be trouble arising in some other piece of classic literature? The thought that I might be entirely on my own this time was a little disconcerting, but I would figure it out. Matthew needed to be with Cooper. Those two had so much lost time to make up for.

"Charles."

I recognized that deep, sexy voice. I'd been so absorbed in my thoughts that I hadn't even heard him approach. I tried to put on a detached expression before I faced him, but I simply couldn't do it. I was smiling through my tears as I walked toward him.

"I love you." He mouthed the words.

Before I could say them back, he was gone. I reached a hand toward the bars, but then I felt faint.

I FOUND myself standing alone in a forest. The first thing I did when I'd gathered my wits about me was to see if the dress I was wearing had pockets. It did. In one pocket, there was a note. I unfolded it and read:

My darling, Gia:

How can I ever thank you for what you've given Cooper and me? He is fine, by the way, and sends you his love and gratitude. He did not have a stroke. He was suffering from

Lyme disease, and that caused his temporary facial paralysis. He has since made a full recovery.

Your wedding ring is here safe and sound. A Tale of Two Cities *has reset, and all is as it should be with the manuscript.*

In case you haven't figured it out yet, you're in Lewis Carroll's Alice's Adventures Under Ground. *I'll be joining you soon.*

I love you,

Matthew

The letter disintegrated as soon as I read it. I supposed it was up to me to determine what to do next— find a mystery that needed solving, I guessed.

Gazing around, I saw a large, yellow-eyed tabby cat perched in a tree. I stepped closer to get a better look.

The cat smiled. *"Eh, bonjour!"*

I threw back my head and laughed. "Oh, Vidocq, you are incorrigible."

ALSO BY G. LEESON

Have you read the prequel to the series, SAVING PIGLET? If you haven't but would like to do so, please visit this link: https://dl.bookfunnel.com/4i9dt3pxir

Have you read book one in the series, **AN EYRE OF MYSTERY?** If you haven't but would like to, you may buy it from the Books2Read link at many retailers (https://books2read.com/u/mqE0ye), at Amazon (https://www.amazon.com/dp/B09ZDLM7B7), or you may read the first five chapters here (https://dl.bookfun nel.com/fkduqmzgrk).

ACKNOWLEDGMENTS

I'd like to thank Shannon, Michelle, Eleanor, Larry, Benjamin, Jessica, and, of course, Zoltan who helped inspire An Eyre of Mystery at the Smithmore Castle Writers Retreat in 2021. Thanks, too, to fellow writers Jennifer, Melissa, and Erin for being sounding boards and to my wonderful family for believing in me even when I'm ready to give up writing altogether and go to work for Spirit Halloween (which I think would be really fun if I could just get paid for dressing up and playing with Halloween props). Last, but certainly not least, if you're looking for some amazing cover art, check out covervillain.com.

ABOUT THE AUTHOR

G. Leeson might appear to be new to writing, but she's better known as Gayle Leeson. As Gayle Leeson, she writes cozy mysteries; but a marketing expert warned her that cozy readers might not follow her into the portal fantasy realm. She, on the other hand, will read just about anything. If you'd like to see what else Gayle has written, please visit her website at https://www.gaylelee son.com/.